Outlandish Affairs

An Anthology of Amorous Encounters

introduced and edited by

EVAN ROSENTHAL
and
AMANDA ROBINSON

Luath Press Limited

EDINBURGH

www.luath.co.uk

*Special thanks to
Alan Jamieson and Dilys Rose*

First published 2004

The paper used in this book is recyclable. It is made from
low-chlorine pulps produced in a low-energy, low-emission manner
from renewable forests.

Printed and bound by
Bell & Bain Ltd., Glasgow

Typeset in 10.5 point Sabon by
S. Fairgrieve, Edinburgh 0131 658 1763

Contents

But love is blind, and lovers cannot see
The pretty follies that themselves commit.

   – William Shakespeare, *The Merchant of Venice*, Act II scene 6

Introduction

WE LIVE IN AN AGE where travel, the Internet and the media have brought us closer together than at any other time in history. As our expansive world shrinks into a global village, cultures inevitably mix and differences are exposed. The results are often awkward, often humorous, always worth retelling.

The general premise behind *Outlandish Affairs* is simple: inspired by the multicultural nature of society and literature, we invited a variety of authors from both sides of the Atlantic to give us their unique takes on cultural difference, in the context of a love affair. Thus the seeds for *Outlandish Affairs* were planted and we then waited for them to sprout. The stories we received were from a diverse selection of up-and-coming writers, peppered with those by seasoned authors, who all skillfully and creatively animated these amorous encounters. Out of the minds of this group, the original idea blossomed into a complete anthology.

Just as the outcomes of these dalliances are unpredictable, so too were the stories that returned from the writers. The collection opens with Scotland-based writer Ruth Thomas's *Bathwater*. Her pizza-chef protagonist, struggling to make conversation with her attractive South American colleague, asks: '...on the other side of the equator, the bathwater goes down the plughole in the opposite direction. Is that true? Do you know? Does it go clockwise or anti-clockwise?'

Former journalist Rob Tomlinson describes a promising media career disappearing down the plughole in *Fade to Black*, where a sexual rendezvous with an Eastern European admirer comes back to interfere with a TV reporter's ambitious plans. On the other side of the pond, in New York City, another reporter gets to grips with dried fish while interviewing a behemoth Icelandic strongman in Marcie Hume's *They Grow the Ice Thick*.

The fine arts are also represented in our stories, along with the confusion that can arise from cultural interpretation. A French artist's dedication to her performance piece frustrates an admirer's intentions in Kate Tregaskis's *Mouse Trap*, while a museum guard has more on his mind than art in *Camille* by Dilys Rose.

Amanda Robinson and Aury Wallington, on opposite sides of the Atlantic, are both concerned about the ambiguous sexual preference of their male characters – although Amanda's story, *Something's Coming* is set in central London while Aury's *Estonia Cowboy Rocks* opens in a smoky bar in Estonia where she admits: 'The purse should have tipped me off.'

Other authors hope to bring together wartime foes: Jewish-American writer Joshua Isard mends the German-Jewish divide in *You Cannot Escape it, You Can Only Hope to Contain it*, while Brian D. Algra's appropriately titled, *A Regime Change of Heart*, brings to life a romantic pre-war interview between a sexy American journalist – 'The Baghdad Bombshell' – and a lothario Saddam Hussein. Age can create as wide a gulf as national difference, as we see in Liz Berry's story *The First Illumination of Lily Lavelle* as the dormant passions of a staid librarian are awakened by a young Hungarian exchange student. In *Shark Attack,* Curt Rosenthal pits predatory Australian sirens against a wizened Italian-American gambler.

Sharks aren't the only creatures astir in the anthology. A pair of Glasgow-based writers focus on cross-species encounters: Aimee Chalmers is bothered by an avian interloper in *The Bird* and Ken Shand strays deeper into the animal kingdom with *Celia, The Seal*: 'For once I had a true true love. Her name was Celia, and she came from the sea, and it was to the sea she returned, as seals, sirenians and other semi-aquatic mammals are wont to do.' In *Braga*, Suhayl Saadi stretches the cross-cultural divide further as he delves into the world of the supernatural, uncovering the mystery behind a haunted rectory in Orkney. Evan Rosenthal hints at the relationship between human and the divine in *The Flight of the Weatherman*, telling the story of an small-town girl's encounter with a weatherman's God complex (or quite possibly God's weatherman complex).

Outlandish Affairs features a wide variety of authors who each have a unique perspective on cross-cultural encounters. The stories range from the tragicomic to the simply perplexing and illuminate the unique problems and possibilities we face at the start of the new millennium. Above all, these stories aim to entertain. Enjoy!

Evan Rosenthal
Amanda Robinson

BATHWATER

Ruth Thomas

BATHWATER

Ruth Thomas

THE OTHER MORNING, Pietro came into the restaurant and put his arms around me.

'Did you know you've got flour in your hair?' he asked.

'I always have flour in my hair.'

'It makes you look like an old lady.'

'Thanks.'

'A pretty old lady.'

Up close, Pietro smelled of onions and Davidoff.

'You seem a bit down,' he said.

'Do I?'

And I thought I had been disguising it very well. I thought nobody would notice that I've been walking around with a heart as heavy as a rock. Or a lump of dough. That I'd been staring into the stainless steel mixing bowl and seeing nothing but hopelessness. Dough and hopelessness.

'Would you like to meet up one evening? Maybe Friday?' Pietro asked.

'Okay,' I said, thinking that his arms felt quite nice around my shoulders – a gentle weight – 'why not?'

Which was the moment I decided to invite him round for a meal. You'd think I'd have had enough of cooking. And of men. 'Glutton for punishment,' my mother would say.

On Friday the doorbell rings at seven. I have just got out of the bath – patchouli-fragranced – and wrapped myself in a largish hand-towel, and for a second I wonder – I hope – that it is not Pietro but another man, Colin: the man I really love, the man I am in love with, who left me two weeks ago to live in Birmingham. But it isn't. My heart flops a little as I open the door a few inches to reveal two adolescent boys. A short one and a tall one. The short one is wearing a black T-shirt and a knitted hat, pulled low over his eyes. The tall one is wearing a hooded jacket and standing a little way behind him, in the darkness of the corridor.

'Hi there,' the short one says tragically, 'Don't worry, I'm not trying to sell you anything. We're just in the area with this amazing promotion. Do you like pizza?'

'It's okay,' I say, hiding behind the door, aware of my nakedness beneath the towel.

'Well, Pizza Pizzazz have got this amazing offer,' the boy drones. His Adam's Apple is enormous. He holds out a clipboard and a laminated sheet which has photographs of pizza slices. The mozzarella strands look like shark's jaws.

'Do you like pizza?' he asks again.

Behind him, the tall boy makes a sighing noise and shifts his weight from one leg to the other. There is a curious smell of pine, like the stuff I use to clean the bath.

'For £20 you can – ,' the short boy says, and I interrupt him.

'I'm sorry, I'm a bit pushed for time.' Also, I am standing here wrapped in a handtowel.

'But surely you have time for pizza?' the tall boy says sadly. 'Everyone likes pizza.'

'I do. But I make it myself. I work in a pizza restaurant.'

The boys stand and look at me.

'I make pizza dough,' I add.

'Fair enough,' the tall one says.

'Right,' says the short one.

He looks depressed, the plastic sheet swinging in his lowered hand. The two of them turn and begin to plod up the stairs and I shut the door.

I never thought I would say that one day: *I make dough*. 'You just don't earn much,' Pietro said the other day, on his way through to the kitchen. And then he winked. Pietro is the head waiter. He wears Brylcreem in his hair, and I am not sure I like him very much, despite his nice brown eyes. Still, here he is, coming round for supper. I do these things. I think maybe they will help to mend my heart.

By seven fifteen I am a little more prepared. But not too much. I have the wine open, the make-up bag unzipped, the vase of flowers perched on the little side-table in the living-room. And dinner is assembled. For the first course there is my specialty: fanned avocado slices with warm redcurrant jelly – nicer than it sounds. For the second course there are lamb chunks, peppers and onions on skewers. For pudding there is Pavlova. I bought some Meringue Nests and piled cream and raspberries into them. I am really not so interested in Pietro that I will beat egg whites for quarter of an hour.

The doorbell rings at seven thirty. Surprisingly it is Pietro. I have not even put on mascara or combed my hair. But he still tells me I look nice.

'Yeah, right.'

'You do.'

'Yeah, right.' Since losing in love I have also lost the ability to be gracious.

Pietro has brought me a big bunch of early daffodils, their petals a delicate yellow, their trumpets powdery and scented. 'Thanks,' I say, wedging them into the only vase I have; a knobbly ceramic thing that is supposed to look like a tree-stump. My landlord has the most hideous collection of china.

I have decided that it would be a mistake to dim the lights or put candles on the table or play gentle music, so we sit down beneath the light of a hundred watts and listen to some Reggae on my cassette player. My hamster, Fluffy, spins frantically around in his wheel in the corner of the room.

'How was the restaurant?' I ask, for something to say. I put my hand up to my hot cheek.

'Busy,' Pietro replies, looking rather sadly at the daffodils, and probably thinking they would look much prettier in a different vase, under a more flattering light. He still smells of Davidoff but not so much of onions. His breath is Listermint-fresh.

'Was it a pasta or a pizza day?' I ask. Because some days everyone goes for pizza and others, often rainy days, they all want the linguine or the penne alla pesto.

Pietro considers. 'Pasta,' he says. 'A lot of spaghetti.'

Occasionally we look into each other's eyes, and maybe there is a little spark there; I'm not sure – I can't tell anything about romance any more.

'Right,' I say.

The avocados are not as ripe as they could be, as I only bought them two days ago and had to roll them fast between my hands to get them to soften. But Pietro cuts at them politely with his fork and tells me the first course is very nice – a very unusual combination of ingredients.

'You're a good cook,' he says. 'Maybe you should set up your own restaurant.'

'You need cash to do that.'

'Dough!'

'Indeed.'

'Maybe you could get a bank loan.'

'Hmm,' I say, pushing bits of stringy avocado around my plate and wondering how long Pietro is planning to stay. I am tired. I glance at my watch. It is seven forty-five. I want something else to happen. I want Colin to be sitting here. 'But is there room for another restaurant in Portobello?' I drone.

'You can't work in Luigi's for the rest of your life. How old are you?'

'None of your business,' I say, my words failing to come out as high-spirited and coquettish as I intended. 'Anyway. That's enough about me.' Now I am in a flippant mood; possibly a mean mood. 'How about you? I presume you were born in Italy?'

'No. Argentina.'

'Oh.' I don't know what to say for a moment. I always assumed Pietro was Italian. 'So do you speak Spanish, then?'

'Spanish and Italian. My parents are Italian.'

'Oh. I thought... yes, I suppose... '

Pietro sits opposite me and smiles. He has very nice eyes and speaks three languages fluently. I know several girls who would swoon.

Unfortunately, Colin wasn't in love with me. I understand that now. I was just someone to sleep with from time to time, someone to have conversations with in pubs. We were together, in the way a badly-strung puppet is together, for nearly two years. But there were other women. I used to think he was good-looking. But now I realise his eyes were actually quite small and muddy. He was tall and slim but he had pallid skin and a bit of a pot-belly from drinking too much beer. His kisses often tasted of beer. And two weeks ago he left me. He got in his Fiesta and drove down the MI to Birmingham. Leaving me to wander around with this huge, painful heart.

'So what did you do before you came to Luigi's?' Pietro asks.

'A Philosophy degree.'

'Good vocational choice, then.'

He smiles again; a kind smile. His eyes are not so much 'come to bed' as 'sit on the sofa.' Warm, comforting eyes. I smile back and dab decorously at my lips with my napkin. I tuck a loose strand of hair behind my ear. Something is awakening in me, despite myself; some latent desire to please.

'It's funny,' I say, 'I never realised you were from Argentina.'

'People always assume I'm Italian. It's my smouldering good looks.'

'Yeah,' I say, realising suddenly that he is good-looking; that I am having dinner with a very good-looking man. But a nice man, too; a friendly man. A man who likes me. We are halfway through the lamb kebabs (slightly overcooked) and I am racking my brains to think of something to say, something interesting, maybe something about living in the southern hemisphere, when it occurs to me. I swallow a hard bit of lamb and clear my throat.

'Somebody told me once,' I say, 'that on the other side of the equator, the bathwater goes down the plughole in the opposite direction. Is that true? Do you know? Does it go clockwise or anticlockwise?'

I look at him, and note with alarm the expression of bafflement on his face. And then the doorbell rings.

'Excuse me,' I say. I push my chair back. 'I bet its pizza salesmen,' I call merrily over my shoulder as I walk out of the kitchen, 'I keep getting pizza salesmen!'

But it is not. It is Colin. He is standing there, tall and pale and not in Birmingham. Not in Birmingham. I don't know what to say. I just stand on the doormat and stare, my heart plummeting like a lift.

'Can I come in?' he asks in his voice, and I step back as he floats in, wearing his threadbare coat; the one with the loose left pocket which I darned once, like a doting wife. He heads straight towards the kitchen.

'I – ,' I say, scampering after him. But it is too late.

'Oh,' he says, staring at Pietro. Pietro stares back from the table, a few grains of Basmati rice stuck to his lips. He still looks confused as if he is thinking 'Clockwise or anti-clockwise? Clockwise or anti-clockwise?' There is no sound apart from the noise of Fluffy's teeth gnawing at the bars of her cage. Without another word, Colin turns and strides down the hallway towards my bedroom. He opens the door, walks in and shuts it behind him, leaving me speechless, shaking, caught between the bedroom and the kitchen, between joy and despair.

There is a little silence. Then Pietro says, 'Is that your boyfriend?'

'No. I don't know.'

He frowns. 'Am I in the middle of something?'

'I didn't know he was going to turn up. I thought he was in Birmingham.'

'Oh.'

Pietro looks at his daffodils again, as if wondering whether to rescue them out of the awful vase.

'I think maybe I'd better go,' he says quietly.

'No, Pietro, honestly...'

'It appears you need to sort something out.'

'No, really, it's – '

And then I hear the front door bang. I flinch. 'Hang on a minute,' I say, turning and running back down the hall to my room. But Colin has gone. He has been here for all of two minutes and now he has left again, like a departing ghost. This time, I believe, really is the last time I will see him. Only a kind of electricity hangs in the darkness, along with his scent, the scent of stale beer and old cigarettes and sadness. But I see he has left a note, on my bedside table. It is written in huge letters, in green biro, on the front page of a library book. How arrogant, my friends would say, how egotistical and arrogant.

I came back to see if we could work things out but you obviously have already.

8

Reading it I feel sick. 'I haven't worked anything out,' I say, out loud. But squinting at his huge, theatrical handwriting in the darkness of my room, I do know something; I know enough. I put my hand up to my cheek and feel how warm it is. 'Right,' I say, and I am turning to go back to Pietro, my smile real, my heart open, when I hear him call 'See you then.' And he closes the front door behind him.

I freeze for a second. This was not supposed to happen. This was not the plan. I put the book down, run to the front door and yank it open. I am just in time to see Pietro's left, Argentinian heel vanish around the turn of the stairs, past a whole pile of abandoned Pizza Pizzazz leaflets.

'Pietro!' I shout. Because I find that I am shouting. And then I am running, back into my room again, going to the window and pushing it up. 'Pietro!' I bellow, like some woman in an opera. We didn't even sit in the living room! I want to shout. We haven't even had the Meringue Nests! But he is not going to look round, I know. I watch him walk to the corner of the street, turn and disappear.

Two men, I think, *two men have left me in the space of two minutes. A man a minute.* I shut the window and go into the bathroom. I fill the basin right up to the top, let the water settle, and pull out the plug.

Anti-clockwise. Anti-clockwise in the northern hemisphere.

FADE TO BLACK

Rob Tomlinson

FADE TO BLACK

Rob Tomlinson

FAME. ADULATION. WOMEN. Glamour. In no particular order, it's what comes to mind when you think of a career in TV. Right…? Okay, I'll be more specific, a career *on* TV. That is, performing, acting, presenting, reporting as opposed to operating a camera, or dangling one of those furry, sausage-shaped microphones over people's heads or walking round wielding a clipboard whilst jabbering into a headset.

Fame. Adulation. Glamour. Less than a year into my job as a local television reporter, I realised I was getting none of it, nor was I likely to. Just because my face popped up for thirty seconds or so on the screen most evenings fronting some instantly forgettable news item didn't mean that I was going to be rocketed into instant stardom. And as for women, forget it. Any likely lass with an eye on a meteoric media career would have taken one look round our newsroom and run screaming for the door. Our female staff consisted of either comfy, mumsy types who did the job to help with their kids' school fees or eccentric spinsters who spent their weekends playing lacrosse and grooming their cats. Once in a while we got fan mail. Often it came on notepaper headed 'HM Prison…' Or it was penned in green ink and proclaimed the writer as the Second Coming and the recipient as the anti-Christ.

So it was that one particularly dismal Monday morning in mid-February, I arrived at work still single and with the usual heavy heart. Straight away the news editor summoned me over with his shopping list of stories that would go towards making up our thirty minutes of output later that evening. He was fat, bald and unshaven and sweated heavily through a nylon shirt. His desk was littered with empty plastic coffee cups, a mountain of press releases and newspaper cuttings and a paper plate bearing the remains of a half-eaten bacon sandwich.

'I want you to do a death knock for us on three teenagers who were killed when they nicked a car, lost control on a bend and wrapped themselves round a tree,' he said. '... And if you don't get anywhere with that, I've got an 'and finally' about a dog who sings along to records on the radio... allegedly.'

I sighed inwardly. It didn't get much worse for a Monday morning. 'Death knocks' were every reporter's nightmare. They involved knocking unannounced on the door of someone who'd just experienced a sudden and horrific bereavement and asking them to do an interview about it. 'And finallys' – well, they were just as bad in their own way, being the self-consciously wacky items that were used to round off a programme. Once again, I contemplated handing in my notice when the newsroom secretary (middle-aged, thick ankles, attitude problem) wandered over and handed me a large parcel.

'This arrived for you in the post this morning,' she said with a sniff and walked off.

How exciting. Nobody ever sent me parcels. This one was carefully wrapped in brown paper, my name and work address written out in a florid, artistic hand. I took it to my desk to open it, hiding from the news editor behind my computer screen as I did so. It contained a box packed with bubble wrap. Inside was a little teddy bear, a bottle of half-decent champagne and a card.

Happy Valentine's Day, it said, and then: *I am watching you on the local news every night and thinking you are lovely. My name is Edita and I come from Eastern Europe but now I work here at the* UK. *My job is at the Grand Prix circuit in town. I would love it to meet you.*

She hadn't included an address, just a work number. The whole thing was very odd and, I had to admit, flattering. The racing circuit on the outskirts of the city where I lived was one of the best in the country and played host to major Formula One events as well as the World Superbike Championships. It was a Mecca for ambitious blondes who took office jobs there in the hope of bagging a front seat in the glamorous world of motor sport and, one day, dating a Formula One driver. This 'Edita' woman was almost certainly one of them – a highly-strung, thoroughbred Slavic beauty who no doubt hailed from the darkly romantic city of Budapest or the brooding mountains of Transylvania. And she'd written to me! I had to get in touch... or did I? My euphoria had run away with me and just as quickly the hard-bitten, cynical, journalistic side kicked in. This was a wind-up, wasn't it? People in the newsroom were only too aware of my lack of success in the romance stakes and had obviously cooked up some cock-and-bull wheeze at my expense.

Tactfully, I asked around. Everyone professed either complete ignorance, disinterest or mild amusement. Not one of my colleagues, they swore, was responsible. I also made discreet inquiries with friends over the next couple of days and got the same reaction. I came to the conclusion, perhaps naively, that Edita and my mind's eye image of her, were for real. But there was still caution to exercise before finally picking up the phone and calling her. What were the professional ethics of high-flying young television reporters like 'moi' taking the great unwashed ranks of our viewing public on dates?

'You can do as you like, son,' said the managing editor in his whining estuary accent. 'You're an adult – at least I think you are. But have you ever come face to face with our viewers before? Put it this way, I wouldn't hold your breath...'

I didn't care. I had made up my mind already. I would phone up the mysterious, the... exotic... Edita, and ask her out for cocktails at a chic city centre bar. I picked up the phone and dialled, to be greeted by the sing-song tones of one of the receptionists at her workplace.

'Hello, I'm trying to contact a member of staff at the race circuit,' I said, not sure whether to sound formal or friendly. 'I only have the name Edita...'

There was a pause.

'Edita...?'

'Yes, that's right. I'm afraid I don't have her surname.'

'Er... I'm sorry but I can't think of anyone of that name who works here...'

I could hear a loud droning sound in the background. I assumed it was the distant noise of racing cars or bikes doing test laps. Then the receptionist broke in again.

'Ooh... actually... I think I know who you mean... yes, yes, I can see her... I'll have to go and get her... I can't put you through to any extension.'

After a few seconds the distinct hum in the background stopped, there was the sound of footsteps and then, a new voice at the end of the phone.

'Allo... this is Edita speaking...' The voice was deep, certainly European, and, I fancied, sultry.

'Hi... hi,' I said, wondering now how to introduce myself. 'It's Rob here... from the TV?... You sent me a parcel... I was just ringing to say thank you very much.'

'That is okay Rob... I like to give things to people I... what is the word?... *admire*.' She sounded remarkably self-assured and unflustered – more so than I did.

'Well you said in your card you'd like to... to... to meet. I... I was wondering if you'd like to go for a drink... perhaps... one evening... maybe?'

This was ridiculous – why was I the one that was nervous?

'Yes... yes...Wednesday night, Bar Revolution at eight.'

'Wait... wait... I don't even know what you look like...'

'No problem... *I* know what *you* look like... Bye bye, Rob.'

Wednesday night couldn't come soon enough. She had chosen one of the most happening new bars in town for our date. It had been done out in a Soviet revolutionary theme and sold rare Russian vodkas as well as a huge range of beers and spirits from across Eastern Europe. I had visions of her walking through the dark city streets to meet me, her breath condensing in spirals in the cold night air, her lips glossed scarlet, the tresses of her long blonde hair tucked into a hat of blue fox fur, a sable overcoat swishing round her ankles, as her high-heeled knee-length boots of black leather clicked along the pavement...

I arrived at the bar in good time and ordered an extremely expensive glass of beer. There was nothing to do now but wait. I chose a high stool by the window and flicked through a magazine from the bar's large selection of international newspapers and glossies. Eventually she arrived. She must have been over six foot in her heels, svelte, sultry, lustrous, blonde hair, cheekbones to die for, swathed in a stylish leather overcoat and cashmere scarf. I watched her lasciviously as she walked towards me... and continued watching as she walked right past me towards a smooth stockbroker type who she threw her arms around and kissed full on the lips. I turned away in disgust and continued practising the art of trying to read a magazine in a casually distracted manner. Ten minutes later, I was halfway through an item about people who stalk celebrities when there was a heavy tap on my shoulder. I turned round.

'Rob... I am Edita... pleased to meet you.'

She seemed to have appeared out of nowhere, which was just as well for her sake, because if I had seen her coming, I'd have just run.

This was a colossus of a woman, a bull-necked Slavic Amazon with a shock of closely cropped raven hair and the faint outline of a downy moustache in the same hue. As she took off her overcoat I could see the fabric of a gaudily coloured blouse struggling to contain the ripple from her biceps and the heave of her giant breasts, somehow held into position by an industrial-sized bra which groaned and creaked at her every motion. She extended a forearm like a ham shank and enveloped my hand in her meaty palm.

'You like another drink?' She asked, seeing my empty glass. Oh yes, could I use another drink...

'Thank you. I'll have a beer please,' I said smiling, my face contorted in a combination of fear and wonderment.

While she got the drinks, I weighed up my options. I could either leave right there and then, slip out while she wasn't looking and hope she didn't come after me (after all, she only knew where I worked, not where I *lived*)... or... accept her for what she was, put the whole thing down to experience and get legless drunk. What the hell, I'd come this far. I opted for the latter. She caught my eye as she stood at the bar and grinned, the spotlights overhead illuminating a dark brown, hair-covered mole on her chin.

She tottered back over towards me with a tray bearing two vast steins of beer, two shot glasses containing what I assumed was vodka and a large dish of pistachio nuts.

'This is *pivo*,' she said, pointing at the beers. 'Czech beer – it is very, very good. And this...' she pointed at the shot glasses... 'this is plum brandy which we drink all the time where I come from. Is very good for the heart.'

'Where is it you come from?' I asked, realising already that I was beyond the point of no return.

'First you drink the brandy, then I tell all about me. What is it you say...? Down in one...' She motioned to the shot glasses. I closed my eyes, screwed up my face and necked the noxious stuff, immediately reaching for a swallow of beer to chase it down before I gagged. Edita did the same, wiping her mouth with the back of her hand.

'I am from Slovakia, from a city called Bratislava,' she said cracking a pistachio and flicking it into her mouth before tossing the shell over her shoulder. 'Have you heard of this place?'

'Er... yes, yes,' I said uncertainly. What I knew about Slovakia, you could write on the back of a postage stamp. I seemed to recall that it was the less desirable bit of what used to be Czechoslovakia and remembered a recent football match in which its national team had come perilously close to embarrassing England.

'I love my country... it is very beautiful,' she went on, all misty-eyed. 'But I have to move to get on in my life... there is no work for me there... there is no... how you say...?'

'Prospects?' I suggested, taking another large draft of beer, my throat still stinging from the Slovakian firewater.

'Yes... yes... prospects... that is it.' She cracked four or five pistachios, threw the shells on the floor again and palmed the nuts into her mouth before draining her ale.

'It sounds like you're doing well over here in England though,' I offered, trying to sound encouraging. 'Working at the race circuit must be very glamorous and exciting. What is it you do? I suppose you're on the admin or secretarial side?'

'Rob... I do not want you thinking badly of me...' She'd come over all doe-eyed. 'But what I do... it is not very much what I do... not very good.'

'Well I didn't expect you to be a Formula One driver,' I said, smiling.

'First I get another drink, then I tell you...'

'No... no it's my round. What would you like – the same again?'

'Yes – beer. And don't forget the plum brandies.'

I duly obliged. We necked the brandies once again, cooled our throats with the beer and she continued.

'So, you wanna know what I do at the race track?' she asked. I nodded. 'I am a cleaner,' she said, looking crestfallen. 'Each day I polish floors and vacuum' (that would explain the strange droning noise when I called her), 'I empty bins, I dust.' Her sadness was gradually turning into a powerful anger. 'I empty stinking ashtrays, I pick up other people's rubbish and I scrub their shit and piss from the toilets. That is what I do – all for... for... for...'

'A pittance?' I suggested.

'Yes – that is it! A pittance!' She cracked more nuts, flicked them one by one in to her mouth, drained her stein and requested more beer.

'Well it's a job and someone's got to do it,' I said weakly, realising this was a woman who wouldn't be mollified easily.

'Do you know what it's like working with piss and shit and filth all day, Rob?' she asked as I came back from the bar with another round.

I certainly did not. I decided to take it as a rhetorical question and tried to change the subject.

'Can I ask why you decided to write to me at the TV station?' I said, downing my brandy without flinching this time and taking a hefty swig of Czech ale. Her expression softened.

'Because I thought you have ability to help me,' she said, smiling. I gulped. She went on. 'You have very sweet face, like little boy. When I see you on TV, I want to care for you. Because I can see that you care about others, Rob.'

What? I nearly choked on my beer.

'When you do the sad stories on the news, you too look sad. When you do the happy stories at the end about fluffy animals and children, you too look happy.'

She'd completely fallen for my sham of a TV persona: hook, line and sinker.

'But I could make you really happy because deep down I can see that you are sad. You are sad and lonely. In my country, women care for men still. Not like here in England. I want to cook and clean for you, Rob – make a home for you to come back to at night. That way I help you, you help me. We make good home for each other.'

She went to the bar to get yet more drinks and as I looked at her this time from a distance, she was looking oddly attractive. I decided right there and then, my beer goggles by now firmly in place, that I would have this creature if she were willing. I would grapple with this woman-mountain, conquer her and give her the ride of her life. In fact by now, I was taking perverse pleasure in the thought of peeling off her clothes and navigating my way around the peaks and troughs of her muscles. She was the living, breathing embodiment of the female Eastern block shot-putting stereotype – and yet I might be able to tame this rugged, hirsute beast...

My next clear memory is of waking up in my flat, turning over in bed and seeing Edita's huge bulk beside me, one of her chunky arms, dusted with dark downy hair, draped across my stomach.

I say *clear* memory because I also had a very hazy one of her singing Slovakian gypsy folk songs in my kitchen while we finished a bottle of Mexican mescal which I'd been trying to get rid of for seven years – and I believe that night I drank the worm. Or maybe it was her.

My hangover lasted for five solid days. It had taken a lot of diplomacy and persuasion to get her out of the flat, along with sworn pledges that I would contact her again. But my immediate concern was for my liver and brain – vital organs that had perhaps been irreparably damaged by the onslaught of alcohol that night. I flopped around for several days, barely able to walk for the hammering in my brain, able to stomach only bread and milk. Eventually I had the guts to look down and examine my nether regions – my sacred private parts were a mess of bruising, red welts and teeth marks. God alone knew what had occurred down there. I phoned work to tell them that I had been run over by a truck and then attacked by a wild animal as I lay in the road injured.

Then she started with the phone calls. Somehow she'd got my home number, mobile number, pager – the lot. I answered the first couple and promised I would be in touch when I got better. I never did and the calls persisted. I ignored the first few but they kept coming. One rain-swept Monday I was awoken by the phone at 6.30 in the morning. I resolved to put an end to it once and for all and snatched up the receiver in a fit of temper.

'Yes!!!?' I bellowed.

'It's me, Edita,' she sounded all sheepish and coy.

'Don't come the little-girl-lost routine with me,' I shrieked. 'Look Edita. I met you, we had a drink, we got drunk, things went a little farther than they should have done and that is the end of it. It should never have happened. I apologise if I led you to believe otherwise. Now will you please leave me alone!'

'You said you wanted to marry me.'

'That is a lie.' (Oh my God, did I?)

'You asked me more than once for my hand in marriage. You got on your knees and begged. In my culture, that means we are betrothed... I think that is what you say... yes, that is it we are... engaged.'

I slammed the phone down in horror. The only policy now was to go completely to ground. I would 'maintain radio silence' as they say. The coward's way out. I got into the habit of not answering the door. All telephone calls were screened. My answering machine was on permanently. Her calls grew more menacing – abuse, violent tirades, death threats even. Then there was the stack of mail that piled up, the envelopes written in an increasingly crazed hand. I stuffed them into the bin. Mercifully, she never came round to my flat. When I returned to work there were letters and calls there as well. Three or four times a day my direct line would ring. I'd pick it up to silence, then I would hear the sound of a loud vacuum cleaner or sometimes a toilet chain flushing, followed by more silence and then the dialling tone. The bemused newsroom secretary would approach with yet more letters. I had gone from getting no personal work mail to daily letters. I hadn't got the courage to explain to my colleagues the sudden burst of popularity – couldn't tell them why I'd finally got the adulation I'd craved. Eventually I cracked; I decided to open one of the letters at random. The opening line really freaked me:

So Rob, it read. *You got to fuck the fat girl.*

And then you toss her aside like a dog that is tired of a bone. One day you might forget me but I never forget you. You go on to fame and fortune with your TV job and I will carry on scrubbing and cleaning other people's shit and piss and dirt...

Yes, I thought, dismissively. That is exactly what I'll do, knowing, logically, that one day the calls and letters would stop and that she would fade from my memory and I would fade from hers. It would be a lesson learned for both of us. And, for just over a year, that is exactly what happened.

By the following Spring I was still working at the same TV station but I knew my days there were numbered. I'd worked hard over the past year and had interest from one or two of the big players in London who'd responded well when I'd sent them my showreels. I had interviews and meetings lined up at Sky, ITN and the BBC with tacit offers. Since I'd finally lain the ghost of Edita to rest my love life had taken a turn for the better as well. I was dating a leggy and ambitious young production assistant from the office called Inga (her mother was Swedish) who, for some reason, thought I was the best thing since sliced bread.

One warm May morning the news editor called me over offering me an assignment that had the potential to launch me into the national spotlight.

'As I'm sure you know, it's the start of the British Grand Prix at the race circuit tomorrow,' he said. 'There's a big press launch with a chance to film all the drivers warming up today and do all the interviews with the top names. The London office was sending one of their guys up to cover it for the whole of the national TV network but he's gone sick at the last minute. They've asked me if you'll do it.'

'What?' I said, incredulous.

'Yeah – it's your big chance this one Rob,' he went on. 'They want live inserts into all the network bulletins nationwide, fronted up by you. If you make a good job of it, your future in the business could be guaranteed. But you'd better get your skates on. Your first live piece is scheduled for their next bulletin in an hour and a half's time. They've got a satellite truck and a cameraman, ready and waiting for you. All the interviews with the celebs and the drivers are already lined up.'

The next hour or so went by in a whirl as I gathered my thoughts, got down to the race circuit and went through the intro into my first live insert time and again until it was word perfect. Inga had come along with me as my general gofer. The first piece I was to do was set for eleven o'clock. By ten minutes to the hour I was in position ready and waiting. The plan was that the camera would start on me sitting in the cockpit of one of the Formula One racing cars. I would do an initial spiel, climb out, walk round the car, talking a bit more about the event as I did so, the camera would pan round to show the viewers the circuit and then I would be joined by one of the leading drivers for a brief interview. The whole item was to last no more than two and a half minutes. But it was two and a half minutes that could set me on the road to fame. With two minutes to go to air, my earpiece was in and I could hear the producer and director in London talking to me. Out of the corner of my eye, I could see Inga giving me the thumbs up. The racing driver was standing next to her waiting patiently to be interviewed.

'Okay Rob. With you in a couple of minutes, love,' said the camp director down my ear. 'Just relax and enjoy it.' Soon my first national broadcast would be beamed by satellite across the nation. I checked my earpiece and my radio mic and clambered into the tight-fitting cockpit of the racing car, ready to go. The cameraman put his headphones on, checked that he was fully cabled up for the live transmission and gave me the 'okay' sign. A small crowd had gathered, as they always seemed to whenever a camera appeared. I was ready to go.

I looked ahead of me down one of the long straights of the circuit to focus my thoughts. Suddenly, out of the heat haze, I saw a figure bounding at a reasonable trot towards my position. It seemed to be carrying a large bucket. Well, as long as whoever it was wasn't going to pass through the shot when we were on air, I wasn't bothered. I looked down and fiddled with the small mic attached to my lapel. Looking up again I could see the figure was still heading my way and getting ever nearer. It was a bulky individual with a look of pure evil in its dark eyes... Christ on a bike!... It was the mad Edita! In all the flurry of the past hour or two, I'd never given her a second thought. It never even occurred to me that she'd still be working at the race circuit. I thought she'd packed her bags long ago and gone back home for a life of domestic bliss with a Slovakian goatherd. But she obviously hadn't forgotten me. Somehow she'd got wind I was there and was coming straight for me with revenge on her mind. My earpiece crackled into life again.

'Okay Rob, with you in twenty seconds now, love,' chirped the director. 'Just remember, relax and enjoy.'

By now she was just yards away from me, the bucket swinging away in the grip of one of her huge hands. Her other hand was balled into a vast fist which she shook at me venomously. The cameraman was oblivious to her approaching from behind and continued to point his lens straight at me in readiness for transmission. I had to get out of the car where I was now a sitting target. But the cockpit was tiny and held me in fast. My cramped legs wouldn't move, my arms had gone to jelly and try as I might I couldn't force myself out of the small space...

'Joining us now from the Grand Prix Race Circuit, with all the latest, here's Rob Tomlinson...'

The anchorman's cheery handover to me was the last thing I heard through my earpiece as a shower of turds, urine and fag ends hit me full on in the face from the bucket. Everyone involved – cameraman, director, producer – was so utterly bemused that the shot lingered on me for several seconds as the hideous mess ran through my hair down my face and into my lap. I stared into the lens, blinking, stinking and speechless.

Finally, after what seemed like a lifetime, I heard the director wail 'Fade To Black! Fade to Black!'

The assembled crowd – the camera crew, Inga, the racing driver and others – looked on in astonishment. As for Edita, she didn't say a word. She just turned right around and sauntered back along the racetrack towards the sun, swinging her bucket and whistling.

Fame? I'd certainly, if briefly, achieved it. Adulation and women? In the shape of Edita, yes. Glamour? It was nearly mine for the taking. Three out of four isn't bad.

As for the rest of my TV career? … It faded to black…

CAMILLE

Dilys Rose

CAMILLE

Dilys Rose

FROM THE BEGINNING I've had to share Camille with countless others but somehow this has never bothered me. In fact, the opposite is true: it adds to her appeal. Observing the intoxicating effects of desire, thirsty eyes drinking in her cool liquid curves, an impulsive hand reaching out, unable to control the urge to touch, it stirs me too but of course, that's when I intervene. It gives me a mean pleasure, I admit, to stop that hand in its trajectory, to step between it and the object of desire, to have such power over so many rivals. Not that I abuse my power. I am at least superficially sympathetic. I understand the motivation to transgress, to cross the boundary between looking and touching but rules are rules and I am paid to make sure the punters stick to the rules. They can look all they want: they have paid for the privilege and some would spend hours salivating over the sleek, small-boned perfection of Camille's body if other interested parties didn't shuffle up behind them and nudge them into moving on.

I first became enamoured with my enduring love, my Camille, during a weekend break in Paris. It was spring. The month of April. April in Paris is a cliché of course but after an especially dreich Edinburgh winter I was not at my most imaginative or adventurous. Grey days, I find, numb grey cells. Not that on the weather front Paris, last year, was much better. One afternoon was dry enough for the whores to prop themselves in doorways around the Pigalle, bra straps and stocking tops flashing beneath shiny, tightly belted macs but otherwise it rained a lot and when it rains a tourist has no option but to seek out some indoor pursuits. In retrospect, I am immensely grateful for those drenching Parisian downpours. Without them, and without one in particular last year, I might never have clapped eyes on Camille. Today, Good Friday, I think of as our anniversary.

At first, on the dry days, I took a passing but eager interest in the fabled Parisian whores. Some of them, in their theatrical make-up, were stunning and scary, like exotic, fiercely coloured plants or insects. But even in the youngest, most immaculately presented specimens I could detect the beginnings of decay – a tightness around the mouth, a clouded gaze. And I only had to look along the street at some of their older associates to see how life would brown their edges, turn their glossy hair to straw, their blemish-free porcelain skin to crackle ware.

I did not come to Paris for whores though. I came laden with the naïve and greedy hope that I might meet a woman who would give of herself freely and lasciviously, who would eat me up with her huge French-season-at-the-Filmhouse eyes and spread her endless legs before I'd even thought to ask. But I soon began to wonder just how French women acquired their reputation for sensuality. The ones I met who weren't expecting to be paid by the half hour were ice queens who sneered at my school French and smirked at my inarticulate attempts to chat them up. Couldn't they have been a little kinder to an innocent abroad? Where was their sense of hospitality? Stuff them, was my response after a couple of days of humiliating knockbacks. Stuff the lot of them.

My lack of success made me feel almost nostalgic for Jeanette, my ex-girlfriend who, after copious quantities of alcohol, would, on occasion, replace her sober frigidity with drunken passion. One night, in my oppressively dignified pension, contemplating the superfluous bidet in my room, I almost called her with the intention of attempting some verbal stimulation. Just as well the cheap cognac I'd been getting through slowly but steadily knocked me out. Jeannette would have perceived my talking dirty as an insult when it was, in my mind at least, a compliment of sorts. But this isn't about Jeanette. And I don't bear her any grudges. On the contrary. By revealing her shortcomings, Jeannette did me a service. I'm grateful to her. She made me appreciate all the more Camille's glowing, immutable perfection.

The trouble with Jeanette and those who proceeded her was

quite simple. No matter what had attracted me to any of them in the first place, it didn't last. The face, which had looked inviting and alluring in a late night bar, when seen the next morning, creased on a pillow, already betrayed signs of future deterioration. New and startling twists and turns beneath the sheets soon became a wearisome routine. A beguiling personality sooner or later began to irritate. But the worst of it was how deeply unreliable they all were. Not one of them, in spite of their repertoires of endearing little quirks, made any kind of lasting impression.

I took the job here to be near Camille. I moved out of my well-appointed Edinburgh flat, shipped my belongings over and set myself up in a cramped and squalid little one-bedroom apartment in an entirely unremarkable *arrondissement*. A surprising amount of Paris is unremarkable. But where I live is neither here nor there. Camille will never see the place, or judge me on it. Back in Edinburgh, I used to be quite proud of my flat and kept it neat and clean enough for most women's taste – changed the bedsheets regularly, did the dishes, cleaned the toilet, attended to the kind of details some of them get nippy about. I provided a good bed, a good sofa, some artsy erotica on the walls, a decent sound system. Women felt okay about staying over. One or two, including poor misguided Jeannette, briefly entertained the notion of moving in but I soon put them in the picture. No balled tights under the bed or boxes of tampons decorating the bathroom shelf, thank you very much.

The place I have here stinks of the cats which lurk around the landing doing the kind of things cats do, the bed creaks hideously, the toilet's only one step up from a hole in the ground but it's all I need. I have no desire to bring anybody home, least of all Camille. Though I doubt she'd give a toss about the state of my accommodation. She's been around, she's a woman of the world, she knows the spires and sewers of experience. But if somehow we were to be here together, I'm sure that a glass of wine or cognac and a smelly, sexy Gauloise would be all the inducement she'd need to strip off and fuck long into the night.

I have never seen Camille clothed but have concocted many fantasies about what she might wear. Before she takes it off. I've imagined an entire whole wardrobe for my sweet Camille to divest herself of, just for me. Boots, I think, with narrow laces and sharp little heels. A long, hip-hugging skirt. A lacy, semi-transparent blouse, high necked, with lots of hooks and eyes, or tiny buttons. And underneath: frilly, crotchless bloomers, stockings – but of course – and one of those whalebone basques. You can't beat a basque: a garment which displays tits and arse at either end, like pairs of twin spoons and trusses up the flab in between. Whoever invented it was a genius.

My job is not at all well paid, I am obliged to wear a monkey suit and put up with hours of idleness interspersed with idiotic questions day in, day out but I have never once regretted my decision to leave my previous existence and take up a life of servitude on behalf of Camille. To spend my waking hours close to the unclothed, *deshabille* body of my beloved is to live each day in a state of bliss. I have no fear that I will lose her, no nagging qualms that any other man or woman might steal her from me. Many others adore her, of that I am certain, but I protect her well from their advances. I'm always alert to someone moving too close to *mon amour*. That is what I am paid for and I love my work. If it were not likely to arouse suspicion, I would do it for free.

A brain is not required, only a keen pair of eyes, a comfortable stance, a few stock phrases in French, German, Italian, Japanese and a firm and vaguely intimidating demeanour at throwing out time. When I think about what my life consisted of before, the effort required to keep on top of my career, the stresses and strains, the boozing, the fraught nights spent in pursuit of sexual gratification – I must have been mad or just plain stupid. Now, like those hippy dippy spiritual folk I have dropped out of the rat race and found happiness in silent contemplation of my ideal. Now the flames of my desire are fed every second of my working day and I am paid for my untrammelled indulgence.

I know every curve of Camille's body, from the nape of her neck to the arch of her foot. Spending all day in silent contemplation of her assets, I am able to maintain a more or less constant state of mild arousal. Which makes me easy-going and amenable. Which is good for my employers as well as the punters. I am so happy with my situation that I never complain if I am asked to do some little chore not specifically within my remit. In fact, like tonight, on weekends and holidays, I often volunteer to hold the fort, allowing my workmates freedom from the rota to pursue their sad little pastimes. I pity them. They pity me. A reciprocal relationship. They can't understand why anyone would want to coop themselves up in the building when they could be sitting in a café watching *les nanas* on the street or *le foot* on widescreen TV, or traipsing through sodden woods hunting for *champignons*. God, how they bored me last autumn with descriptions of omelettes cooked with chanterelles. At least I keep my pastimes to myself.

There is, of course, security in the building but the directors are very laissez-faire about its deployment. With an elementary grasp of the system and a bit of ingenuity, it's not difficult to find a way of blindfolding the prying eye of a camera. And I do like my time alone with Camille to be private. I can share her for days on end with all those lip-licking oglers but after hours, when I've cleared out the punters, when I've waved goodbye to my workmates as they hurry off, heads filled with their paltry little plans for *le weekend*, when I've bolted the door and set the alarm, she's mine and mine alone.

I draw the heavy curtains, turn the lights off so everything is dark, except for Camille. I leave a spotlight on her. Illuminated, she is an embodiment of the sublime: pale and smooth and flawless, stretched out before me in an attitude of glorious, timeless abandon. I undress slowly. I have waited a long time for this moment when we are alone together but now there is no rush, no rush at all. We have hours and hours together. Undisturbed. I lean over Camille and press my warm, living flesh against her cool immutable perfection.

The initial contrast in temperature, the time and patience it takes to warm her marble breasts in my hands, prolongs my pleasure. I stroke every smooth inch of her, remembering, with a flush of satisfaction, all those other thirsty eyes on her earlier in the day, remembering my polite but insistent request: *S'il vous plait, Monsieur, ne toucher pas.* At this moment I am only jealous of one man: Auguste Rodin, who touched parts of Camille I can never reach.

ESTONIA
COWBOY ROCKS

Aury Wallington

ESTONIA COWBOY ROCKS

Aury Wallington

THE PURSE SHOULD have tipped me off.

I wandered into Levi'st Valjas bar because an ad in the Baltic Times promised 'Straight from America – the Dirty Dog Orchestra' and I was desperate for any sign of home. The venue looked promising enough – a smoky little dive on a cobbled street in Old Town, full of eight foot tall Scandinavians clutching glasses of vodka and dancing on the rustic wooden floor.

Even from outside I could hear the music, a badly butchered Clint Black cover, which I figured was probably just a warm up for the band from the States. But the lead singer, who was wearing a leopard-print cowboy hat and had a face like a hammered plate, finished the song and introduced the band: 'Mart, Tiit, Arnold, and I'm Veljo – ladies and gentlemen, the Dirty Dog Orchestra' and even before he launched into the opening verse of 'Friends in Low Places,' I felt low enough to know that I was the only American thing about this place.

I had finished my student teaching in Brooklyn five weeks earlier, and I wanted to get out of the city for the summer and have a glamorous European adventure before I started my tenure as the newest addition to the P.S.114 English Department. Besides, I had just ended a relationship with a man who turned out to have a wife living on the Upper East Side, and I was desperate to get away from the Bad Relationship Karma. I wanted to have a carefree summer fling, with no strings and no tears, and put the Ex out of my mind.

So I hopped a flight to Estonia, where my older brother Mike, who was a bio-geology grad student, was studying soil samples. I didn't understand why he couldn't study dirt somewhere romantic like Tuscany or the French Riviera, but I figured anywhere was better than Park Slope.

And at first it was great – Estonia is really beautiful, and the town where we were staying, Tallinn, had a bunch of cute stores and cool old churches. And it was nice seeing Mike, now that we were both adults and he was no longer devoting all his energy to tormenting me.

But as the weeks passed, the charm started to wear off. Mike was spending most of his time in Tartu, a little patch of wilderness where there was nothing to do but watch him tweeze microscopic specks of crystal out of the dirt and put them in tiny ziploc bags, for hours and hours at a time. I was pretty much left alone, and as a native New Yorker, I found the solitude terrifying.

So even though I wasn't much of a country music fan, at least the Dirty Dogs were singing in English, instead of the weird runic chanting that was piped in to all the restaurants. And I knew enough of the lyrics to feel a little less homesick, so I took a seat at the bar, ordered a Budweiser which had a freaky Czech label, and watched the Dirty Dogs tear up the stage.

After six more songs, only one of which I recognized as an old Crystal Gayle tune, the band took a break and the lead singer walked over to the bar next to me.

He ordered something that to me sounded like water, but my Estonian is non-existent, so I wasn't too surprised when the barmaid handed him a glass of something brown and syrupy.

'Great set,' I said to him, and his eyes lit up.

'You are American? Welcome to Tallinn!'

'Thanks. I'm Nina.'

He took my hand in both of his and shook it for a long time. 'I am Veljo. We just returned from an American tour. We played at the Grand Ole Opry.'

He looked at me expectantly, so I obliged him. 'Wow! That's so cool.'

'We are only playing covers here tonight for the crowd,' he said. 'I am also a songwriter.'

'Oh, Estonian songs?'

'No way! American! Country!'

'Great,' I told him.

'Do you listen to country music at home?'

No. 'Sure. I mean, I like that 'country roads take me home' song,' I told him.

Veljo grinned, then one of his bandmates called something to him, and he touched my arm. 'I'll talk to you later, yes?'

'Okay.'

Veljo walked away, and I went downstairs to try to find the ladies' room. There were two doors, one marked 'M' for, presumably, Men and the other marked 'N' for... I didn't know. This was the peril of not learning the language. But even though I was studying my Berlitz book every night, Estonian was really hard. And all the other public bathrooms I'd been in were marked with little upside down triangles for men, right-side up ones for women. I hung out in the hallway for a while, until finally a gigantic blond man came out of M. I smiled at him in relief and pushed my way into N.

By the time I got back upstairs, the band was getting ready to start their second set. When he saw me, Veljo jumped off the stage and made a beeline for me.

'Nina. Can I take you to dinner tomorrow?' he asked me, smiling.

I smiled back. 'Let me give you my number.'

I searched through my bag for a pen, but Veljo stopped me. 'Here, I've got one,' and he picked up a purse, the exact same Kate Spade purse I had been coveting for weeks in the window of her store in Manhattan. He dug through his purse, pulled out a pen and a piece of paper, and handed it to me. I wrote down my number at Mike's house and he put it in his pocket. 'I can't wait until tomorrow,' he said, climbing back up on stage. The band started up with 'All My Exes Live in Texas,' and Veljo looked straight into my eyes as he sang.

Yeah. Me neither.

The next night we were sitting at Mookala, drunk on vodka and sharing an enormous platter of what I told myself was sushi, but was really just a big dead fish that we pried hunks out of with tiny serrated spoons, like the type you get at KFC.

'It was Sunday when I got the news, now I got the glasnost blues,' Veljo sang to me.

'Glasnost blues? Are you kidding?' I asked him. I knew Estonia used to be occupied by Russia, but the reference seemed a little dated.

'Shut up,' he said, playfully poking me with his spoon.

I smiled at him, reached across the table and took his hand. 'You might want to make it a little more current if you're going for the big record deal.'

'Maybe I come back to America with you, and get the deal with a hot American chick singing backup.'

'Country rooooooads, take me hoooome,' I sang, and Veljo covered his ears, laughing.

'No, stop, what do you do to Mr Denver?' he said, and took a big swallow of vodka.

I drank some vodka too, put my hand on his leg and gave it a squeeze. I took another sip and smiled at him sloppily.

'I can't believe I only met you now, when I only have two weeks left here.'

'So we are dating for two weeks, then writing love letters forever after,' he told me.

'Nope,' I said, shaking my head. 'You're coming back with me. We could live in Brighton Beach. There's lots of Russians there. They'd know all about glasnost.'

'Pah!' Veljo said something in Estonian that sounded to me like a bunch of owls hooting, then drained his glass and motioned to the waitress to bring us more.

Then he leaned across the table and took my cheeks in both his hands and gave me a careful perfect kiss on my lips. His mouth was cool, and I could taste the raw fish on his tongue. I kissed him back for a minute and when we pulled apart, I already wanted to be kissing him again.

'I like America. The men with their big cocks,' he said.

Excuse me? I shook my head to clear away some of the vodka. 'What?'

'I like the big cocks,' he repeated, then pulled me to him and kissed me again, harder, not even stopping when the waitress set another carafe of vodka on the table with a bang.

'Dude, he's gay,' Mike said, barely looking up from the bags of dirt he had spread out all over the coffee table.

'But he kissed me. Twice in the restaurant and once when he dropped me home. Plus he grabbed my boob when he was saying goodnight.'

'He likes big cocks,' Mike said, laughing. 'I don't think there's a whole lot of room for discussion.'

'But he asked me out for Saturday,' I said, flopping down on the couch next to him. 'He wouldn't want to date me if he were gay. And I don't want to go home without having some wild romantic fling.'

Mike didn't answer me, so I picked up the remote and started flipping through channels. I stopped on MTV Cribs – in Estonia! – and looked over at my brother. 'Maybe he's bi.'

'If it makes you feel better to think he's bi, then go right ahead.' Mike carefully tweezed a tiny glinting stone out of the dirt and smiled at me. 'I just think, no matter how many girls he's banged, if a guy likes cock –' he dropped the stone into a Ziploc bag '– he's gay.'

'Maybe it was a language barrier,' I said. 'He called a knife a 'bowl' earlier. Maybe he thinks a cock is something different than it actually is.'

'Yeah, that's probably it,' Mike agreed. 'Your gay boyfriend is just bad at vocabulary.'

Our plan for Saturday was to take a sauna, which is a terribly Estonian thing to do, and which I'd been leery of trying on my own, because it sounded vaguely sordid to me, like visiting a massage parlor in New Orleans or something.

I needn't have worried.

The locker room was full of fat naked ancient women, all plucking hairs from various parts of their bodies with tweezers. I had brought a bathing suit since I wasn't sure of the protocol, but even though no one else was wearing one I decided to opt for modesty and slipped it on before heading out to the sauna.

I pushed open the door, and it was a tiny cedar box, barely large enough for the two of us. Veljo was already there, sitting on the bench with a towel around his waist, head thrown back against the wall. He opened his eyes when he heard me come in, and gave me a crooked smile.

'You like?'

The heat? Or his perfect muscular bare chest? I chose the latter, and nodded. 'Definitely.'

I sat down next to him, a little woozy, and also closed my eyes. We relaxed, comfortably silent. I was quickly turning into a puddle, but when we'd barely been there ten minutes, Veljo grabbed my hand and pulled me to my feet.

'Nina. We take the plunge.'

He pulled me out the door and, before I knew what he was doing, launched me off the side of a pool into the iciest water I have ever encountered. I felt my heart stop, the shock of the hot to cold making me go into instant cardiac arrest. I couldn't catch my breath, I was sure I was going to drown, but before I could get my mind around it, Veljo was already hauling me out of the water.

He shook himself like a puppy, laughing and giving me a hug, and a wrinkled attendant shoved paper plates of cabbage stew into our hands.

'Wha...?' I finally managed to get out, still overwhelmed from the shock, but Veljo just smiled, already shoveling the food into his mouth.

'Brisk,' he told me.

Yeah, I'd already figured that out.

After we got dressed, we walked down the little path from the baths to his house. He captured my hand in his as we walked, and even though the ice water had left me feeling pretty unsexy, I was willing to give it another chance.

But when we got to his house, someone else was already there. Not another woman, but another man. A cute, mostly-naked, nineteen year old boy, to be precise.

Okay, so he was gay.

The boy was sprawled on the couch, watching TV and leafing through a magazine that had a picture of Courtney Cox on the front. He was wearing a tiny pair of bright red bikini underwear and nothing else, and didn't seem at all surprised to see Veljo and me come in. They hooted at each other for a minute, then the boy got up and went into some back room, and Veljo sat me down on the couch and immediately started kissing my neck.

'Wait –' I said. 'Who was that kid?'

'That was Frank.' Veljo untied the straps of my sundress and moved his hands down to cover my breasts.

'But, who is he?' I wrapped my hands around Veljo's neck, caught his earlobe with my teeth.

Veljo moaned and eased me down on my back, pulling my dress away and kissing down my stomach. 'He is boyfriend,' he murmured. 'He is just visiting.'

Um. I had a follow up question, but I couldn't think of it – I was distracted by Veljo, who put his mouth on the crotch of my panties and blew a hot breath through them. I moaned, arching my back and lifting my hips enough so he could drag them off me. My moan turned into a gasp as he got his mouth on me, invaded my borders, conquered my territories with his lips, set up some peace treaties with his tongue.

I forced my eyes open, looked at his dark hair against the Nordic summer whiteness of my thighs. Veljo quickened his pace, so I let my head fall back on the couch cushions, and saw the boy, now dressed, tiptoeing past.

He saw me notice him and grinned, putting a finger to his lips and winking at me as he made his way out the front door. Jesus Christ.

I sat up quickly, and Veljo raised his head to look at me.

'You are okay?' Veljo asked.

'Um, listen. Wait, stop that and listen for a second.'

Veljo pulled himself up next to me, smiled. 'Yes?'

'So, Frank. He's... he's your boyfriend?'

Veljo nodded, biting playfully at my nipple.

'Wait, so – are you bi? Or, I mean, gay?'

Veljo leaned over and gave me a long slow kiss, then pulled his head away and looked at me. 'Can you taste yourself?'

Oh, god, gross. 'Yeah.'

'Does that mean you are lesbian?'

What? 'No, but –'

'Then shut up and let's fuck,' Veljo said, grinning, and he picked up his purse and rummaged through it for a condom.

'Thanks for coming with me,' I told Mike.

'Are you kidding? I wouldn't miss seeing him for the world.'

All of Tallinn turned out for the Victory Day/Jaanipaev holiday, and Veljo's band was playing in the plaza in Old Town as part of the celebration. I thought I'd have to beg Mike to come with me, since he never seems to be interested in anything that happens above ground. But after telling him what happened at Veljo's, leaving out some of the parts I wouldn't necessarily want to get back to our parents, Mike was dying to meet Veljo and decide for himself if he was gay. Because at that point, I had no idea.

We pushed our way through the crowds and past the bonfires until we got to the annex where the Dirty Dog Orchestra was set up. People were selling Saku Originaal beer out of gigantic Igloo coolers, and as Mike paid for a couple, I saw Frank in the crowd, staring up at the stage and waiting for the band to start. He caught my eye and waved happily, shouting something incomprehensible at me. He seemed so at-ease, while I was so on-edge it was a miracle my hair didn't burst into flame. But I couldn't give him any more of the upper hand than he had already claimed, so I just waved back, then elbowed Mike and gestured with my beer bottle.

'That's the boyfriend,' I told him. But as Mike craned his neck to look, the band came on the stage and, as they launched right into their first number, I pointed Veljo out.

Mike looked him up and down.

'Definitely gay.'

'What do you mean?'

'Nina. He's singing a Patsy Cline song.'

True. 'That doesn't mean anything.'

'But look at how he's dressed. Leather pants? Come on.'

'Hey, you're dressed more gay than him.'

Mike looked down at himself. He was dressed in a classic field scientist outfit – short khaki shorts with a T-shirt tucked in, hiking boots with an inch of sock showing above the ankle – he looked like Bronski Beat.

'Shut up,' Mike said. 'You suck.'

'No, you suck.'

The band finished the song, and Mike and I stopped fighting to hear what Veljo was saying into the mic.

'I sing this next song for my very special lover tonight.'

Moment of truth. I saw Frank glance over at me, his smile gone, and I realized that this was the defining moment, this was when I would know the answer. Was I the special lover or was Frank? The rest of the crowd seemed to fade, leaving just me and Frank, facing each other down. I had no weapon but desire, and the beer I was drinking couldn't disguise the taste of dust in my throat. The music started, a few bars of something I didn't recognize, and I held my breath, waiting for the big reveal. Gay boyfriend or straight boyfriend, what was it going to be?

Veljo leaned into the microphone, and his mouth was so perfect, was such the stuff of fantasy, that my heart sank. I might as well have packed my bags and taken the next flight back to New York. Frank had beaten me; it was over. But then Veljo opened his mouth and started to sing.

'Almost heaven, West Virginia, Blue Ridge mountains, Shenandoah River...'

I grasped Mike's arm to steady myself, tears welling up in my eyes. He loved me. I relaxed, my hands loose at my sides, a dizzy wash of exhilaration flooding over me. Mike looked at me like I was nuts as I sang along with the chorus, 'Country roads take me home to the place I belong...'

I was in bliss the entire rest of the set, and when the band took a break and Veljo came over to talk to me, I threw my arms around him and kissed him with everything I had. When we broke apart, I couldn't stop smiling, and my voice sounded giddy as I introduced him to my brother.

'Veljo, this is Mike.'

Mike held out his hand, and Veljo's eyes lit up. They shook, and as Veljo dropped his hand, he let his fingertips brush across the front of Mike's khaki shorts. 'All right, America!' he said. 'This is what I'm looking for! Nice big cock.'

Mike took a step back, his eyes flickering from me to Veljo like he didn't know whether to laugh or deck him, and Frank suddenly appeared, slipping his arms around Veljo's waist from behind.

'Okay, see you later, Nina,' Veljo told me, draping an arm across Frank's shoulders. 'We go back to my house tonight –' His eyes shifted to Mike. '– You come too.'

Then the two of them walked away. Mike stared down at me, while I concentrated really hard on my beer bottle.

'Maybe he's not...' he started, but I held up my hand.

'Can you go get me another beer?' I asked him. Mike nodded, and I opened my purse, my Kate Spade knock-off from three seasons ago, and pulled out some money and shoved it in Mike's hand.

Mike walked over to the vendor, and I stood alone in the middle of the celebration, barely conscious of the crowds and laughter and hooting discussion, John Denver taking me home in my head.

CELIA, THE SEAL

Ken Shand

CELIA, THE SEAL

Ken Shand

PERHAPS YOU'D NOT believe me to have been young once, and then in love. If you saw me now, wizened, old, and desolate as Lir, perhaps you'd think me a beggar, though once I was a king. For once I had a true true love. Her name was Celia, and she came from the sea, and it was to the sea she returned, as seals, sirenians and other semi-aquatic mammals are wont to do. My home now is banked by this isle's imagined walls, overlooked by the Forth Bridge and overlooking the sea. I am left here with nothing but its waves, and the few lines I've composed after the style of McGonagal. Oftentimes I catch myself looking out across the frothing waters of the Forth, spotting perhaps a buoy (by which I mean a float) bobbing up and down in the water, and I imagine it to be the sleek silvery head of Celia. Or else I may stand skimming stones across the still waters and think of her and of her strange, slightly fishy smell, her thick waxy pelt. Her whiskers, coated always with dewdrop tears. Or I may see that buoy again and think of it as my heart, bobbing up and down in the free channels of my soul, torn away from me, the cruel flotsam of love. And I may wish that Celia's head, the float, my heart, that triptych of desire, was mine to hold forever, rising up always above the waves of my outrageous misfortune; mine gladly mine and always afloat. Or a head. Or a heart. That metaphor is stretching and it will sometime snap, so I'll rush onward with my tale.

I first met Celia in Edinburgh Zoo. At that time I was married to a woman named Jean, and it was with Jean and my friend Roddy that I stood that day, watching the penguin parade. First came the chinstraps, the emperors and kings. I grew excited as I watched them waddle, and laughed a deep deep laugh. Then came my favourites, the macaronis and rockhoppers, their non-conformist yellow crests shining in the grey afternoon. I am, let me just clarify, a marine biologist of some repute. My paper on sea cucumbers was described as 'thorough', but krill's my expertise. I thus dispensed certain crucial titbits to Roddy and Jean, regarding the dietary habits of penguins and their fishing methods. I asked them if they wanted ice-cream, and it emerged that what was needed was a ninety-nine and two oysters. I like to push the flake in, and suck the ice cream out through the stem of the cone, like a tapered wafer straw. I headed towards the stall while Roddy took Jean to the reptile house. I was expecting them back in a minute or so, after I'd bought the ice-cream, but that was the last I saw of them all day.

I stood alone for half an hour or so, a thin cold stream of Mr Softie's dripping down my hand. It was then I spotted Celia, her dark sympathetic eyes shining out at me through the glass of her enclosure. I pressed my face against the glass and stared in towards her as she lay like Aphrodite, decadent on her side, curving up against an island of rocks. Those I took to be her parents lay back like fat tourists on lilos, drifting about in the water, until I began clapping my hands and honking to attract her attention. She gave what I could only assume was a smile of sympathy, and I felt my heart skip a beat. Her parents, though, seemed unimpressed, straightening up and swimming to join her on the island. I realised then that my attraction to her would only ever be consolidated against authority. I clapped my hands again, and pushed my face against the glass. A little plaque to the side identified them as Norwegian grey seals, and I wondered if I'd commited a social faux pas with my forwardness. Perhaps their Nordic temperament made them disapprove of such behaviour. I waved goodbye to Celia, whose name was on the plaque. That evening the answering machine told me it was staying at Roddy's, and that I wasn't to worry. I made myself a mug of Ovaltine, picked a book off the shelf, and sat up in bed, reading until the early hours of morning. The book I chose was *Seals and Sea-lions of the World*. I felt the first sore pangs of love.

Over the next week or so I visited the zoo often, lingering for a while in front of Celia's enclosure each time. I became a seal sponsor, and was given a car-sticker, bookmark and ballpoint pen, each emblazoned with the motto 'Save our Seals'. I placed the sticker on my bedroom window and used the pen whenever possible. The money helped maintain, to my great delight, Edinburgh Zoo's special Seal-Cam, accessible through the internet, allowing me to watch Celia from four different angles, and even underwater. I watched her swim in fuzzy low resolution, each frame staggering forward, unable to keep up with the swift graceful movements of Celia as she swam to and fro, a stream of bubbles fizzing up from her mouth and nose. Only once did I worry that my behaviour was becoming obsessive. It was on a Friday, and Jean had invited Roddy round for dinner. We were having fish fingers, peas and chips, as usual. I pinged my peas around the plate with my fork, chasing them round like a dog playing football. Roddy stopped shovelling his food and looked across at me with a glint of humour.

'Me and Jean were looking at the internet the other day.' The two of them smiled at a shared joke.

'Were you, now. Anything interesting?'

'Aye well you could say that. Bit of animal porn and that.' Jean began to laugh hysterically and for a moment I worried that they were making fun of me. I felt a profound sense of panic, and watched their expressions, but detected no malice. I laughed with them, to ease the situation. I resolved to try and think less about Celia the seal, that strange bewitching pinniped that held my heart within her smooth-downed flippers, lest my love for her should become my downfall.

I threw myself into work. Tried to obliterate all thoughts of Celia. I wrote a paper distinguishing two different kinds of sea ice algae and started going swimming in the afternoons. It didn't help, much. I only cursed my own inadequacies, my failure to emulate the movements of a seal with my rudimentary breast-stroke. I became depressed, inconsolable. One evening, I made my decision. I knew I needed my Celia. I resolved to head home and tell Jean of my new-found love.

My house was in Stockbridge and I got there by bus. We had a nice enough house; two floors, semi-detached. I whistled a sweet song to myself as I headed up past the swing-top bins, past Roddy's Golf convertible to the frosted glass door. Jean was waiting there, looking nervous and slightly drunk.

'Hello darling,' I said to her. I moved to give her a peck on the cheek, but she stepped backwards, revealing Roddy standing behind her in my dressing gown. I'd known Roddy since primary school, where he used to steal my toys and sell them to me afterwards. He looked just like he did then, tall and menacing with a bully's mean stare.

'Hello.' He answered.

'I wasn't speaking to you. Look Jean, I have some news. I don't know how you'll take it, so it's best if we talk alone.'

'You're not getting in.'

'What?'

'You're not welcome here anymore. I'm getting a divorce.' She seemed to be gathering confidence now and began to laugh. 'Anyone else would have realised months ago, but you're so obsessed... Always sitting there behind a microscope with your bloody plankton.'

'It's krill, darling. Krill are a sort of zooplankton, themselves a...'

The door slammed, and I heard laughter from inside.

I took up residency, secretly, within the department, staying back late to do my research. I kept a mattress there to sleep in at night, after the janitors had left me to it, shaking their heads as I informed them I'd be up 'til morning. My dreams were dominated by thoughts of Celia. I threw myself into work, began publishing more papers than I'd been able to before. The Marine Research Association of Tokyo offered me a teaching post I graciously declined. The department was impressed. But I had, if the truth be told, an ulterior motive. As the year went on, I began making increasingly extravagant demands for equipment, buying up everything I would need to give a seal a good life in an urban environment. Eventually I showed my hand. I had Celia transported to the department, so that I could be with her forever. I could scarcely believe it when she arrived, I had waited so long. She was as beautiful as ever, and made a sweet snorting noise when I stroked her. I could not linger on this, however, and okayed the delivery in a professional manner.

It was a long time before I felt confident enough to declare our relationship public. I decided that the best way to do so was time-honoured, and invited her out for a date, taking her bright enthusiastic eyes for an affirmative. I picked a place I thought Celia, who had trouble dancing and didn't really enjoy films, would like. We went to a sushi bar on Rose Street. You might think we'd have trouble getting in, and we did. The security man, a short bulky fellow, was unequivocal.

'No animals.' I looked him up and down, scornfully. I'd spent the day pushing Celia along in a converted pram. Although I'd shocked a few people, who'd grinned in looking for a baby, this sort of treatment was new.

'I'll have you know that this is my girlfriend.'

'No animals.' It took a large bribe and a promise to use a high chair to get us in.

The place was nice, in a minimalist way. A conveyor belt carried a wide selection of raw fish, seaweed wraps and other delights round the room, while the chefs worked away in an open plan kitchen. We took seats at a table on a balcony, up a flight of bamboo effect stairs. After we were comfortably seated, I ordered up a platter to share and a bottle of saki. Celia munched away at the platter appreciatively. I almost cried with happiness. Once I'd sampled a selection of mackerel and pickled ginger I excused myself to the bathroom, where I wet my hair up into a little quiff and washed my hands. I returned to a scene of utter chaos. The whole restaurant was staring towards the conveyor belt with a mixture of horror and hilarity as Celia, my lovely Celia, bounced and wriggled forward, gulping what she could, crushing all else or knocking it to the floor. One of the chefs was giving pursuit, a look of crazed fury in his eyes.

'Get out. Get ouuuut!' I complied with his wishes, pushing the pram to the counter-side and heaving Celia onto it, then racing fast as I could towards the door. She let a piece of chewed monkfish fall as we made our escape. The security man was blocking the door, but stood aside as the chef grabbed a cleaver.

'You fucking. Fucking... seal fucker!!!' I didn't stop to register my complaint.

The incident made it into the *Edinburgh Evening News*. I knew I was done for. That very night I went into hiding, on this my present dwelling place; an island underneath the bridge, a clear day's view from Queensferry. I had enough money left for certain extravagances, made certain repairs on some ruins I found there and made the place my home. I bought a wet-suit and a little dinghy, so that we could spend time together out at sea. Indeed we had two happy years together, setting up home and living close. Once I felt confident enough to contact a friend at the University, to enquire about my post there. I felt a sense of bitterness when he hung up the phone. Of Jean I heard nothing and wanted less. It was then that I took up the art of poetry, seeking to immortalise the love I'd found. Those were happy, happy times.

It was on a stormy, windy September evening that my bliss was disturbed, by a hard fierce rapping at the door. I hadn't had a visitor, had scarcely conversed with another human soul, in all the time I'd lived on the island. I feared to open it. Yet such was the crashing and the whirling of the gale, such was the spattering and pattering of rain, so tremendous were the thunderclaps outside, I feared to leave anyone out in it. How I wish I'd kept the door shut, and laid down with my Celia. I drew the door back, to reveal a tall figure in a large brimmed hat, one hand grasping a walking stick while the other clutched a leather bag. It was the sort of bag my parents told me the doctor brought babies in. He had a long grey beard and wore a huge Barbour jacket, giving him the appearance of a fairytale wizard. I welcomed him inside.

He followed me into the bedroom, where Celia lay, half asleep. I noticed his eyes take on a strange fire.

'Perhaps,' he said, 'we may discuss some matters in the kitchen.' We returned to the kitchen, where I poured him a whisky, and one for myself as well.

'I should introduce myself. My name is Magnus McManus, selkie-expert, and yours my friend, is but too well known.' I had been trying to work out if his accent was Russian or Welsh, but now surmised him to be Orcadian. This he confirmed in a moment. 'In Orkney, where I was born, we have a great many tales of men like yourself, whose eyes glint with a mad rapture and bewitchment. The attraction of those blubbery sirens is but too well known. The unicorn's horn is but a narwhal's tooth, and the same may be said for the mermaid, a transliteration of man's love for the selkie.'

His words moved me to cry out my love for Celia, for at last I felt I'd found another who accepted my choice of lifestyle. I told him of the games we played, sharing chunks of chewed fish, the way we sang to each other, as we swam beneath the waves, the times we shared naked on the rocks, with only the bright eye of the moon watching over us, and the 23:38 to Dunfermline. He shook his head sadly, sagely, and grimaced.

'This seems a worse case than I'd expected. Does she not become a beautiful maiden, stripping off her skin? Cook for you and tend the house, and be in every way as loyal a wife as a man could want?'

I answered, nervously, in the negative.

'My God man. Then she still wears her cloak.' With this he opened his bag up, and pulled out a cut-throat razor. 'Do you not know that she cannot be properly yours 'til the skin comes off?' He made for the door, but I did my best to restrain him, calling out to Celia and urging her to escape. When he got through the door she was gone. He gave out a sharp guttural curse, and stormed out.

I chased after him, eager to find some sign of Celia, who I presumed to have fled. I looked all around, but there was no sign beyond the little half moons displaced by her fins and tail. McManus, that strange devil, I saw only when he was illuminated by great flashes of forked lightning. I saw him at a vantage point staring out at sea. I saw him crouched, raising pebbles close to his eyes, as if smelling them like a bloodhound. I saw him get a boat ready, and I saw him dragging back on the oars, as he made his way away from my island forever.

I too must leave now, having finished my tale. I hope I have your sympathy, if not your understanding. A mist is growing across my eyes and soon the great and rusty bridge will vanish from me. It is unlikely, I think, that my poetic works will survive. I am contemplating the burning of all of them, even the one I think my masterpiece, 'The Bridge that Ventured Forth'. I shall burn them to ashes, and scatter them to the four winds, for they are nothing without my Celia. Only one work will I leave to posterity; an epigrammatic epitaph of sorts. An epigraph? No that's something else. A new word for an old fool. I hope to carve those last words across the door to my lodging, in memory of a sad and tragic life:

'Here lies a man who was good, not great

Always on time, only now he's late

Yet have ye cheer, don't lamentate

For the love of a seal did seal his fate.'

Adieu, my friends.

MOUSE TRAP

Kate Tregaskis

MOUSE TRAP

Kate Tregaskis

CHLOE LEANS AGAINST one of the chairs, smiling at him, her mouth slack from drink; her lipstick has collected round the outline of her lips giving them the look of something peeled. He boils the kettle and opens the packet of coffee he bought for exactly this occasion. Normally he makes do with instant.

– Milk? Sugar?

He doesn't even know how she takes her coffee.

She shakes her head, takes the top off the black marker-pen she holds in her hand and writes *non merci* in the air flamboyantly. Her body bends over, her hands and hair sweep towards the floor like a puppet taking a bow, but instead of bouncing up again she's seen something. She reaches down and retrieves it from beside the fridge. It's a black plastic container the exact shape in miniature of those covered stair-things that are wheeled against the sides of planes to convey passengers on and off the more expensive airlines. She opens one end of the container and peers inside.

– It's a mouse trap. An ethical mouse trap, to catch the mouse alive... the mouse walks up the ramp, like this... making the whole thing topple and then the door snaps shut...

– Eek, she giggles. Re-setting the door, she returns the trap to the side of the fridge.

The trap has been in position for a week now, but there's still no sign of the mouse. The man in the shop had advised using a Mars Bar as bait; it needed to be something sticky so that it would stay in place at the top of the slope. But it seems this mouse doesn't like Mars Bars.

– Coffee...

He hands her a mug and leads the way into the living room where he puts on a CD. *Air*, they're French; she probably likes them. 'Moon Safari', it's their first album; he keeps meaning to buy the second one but hasn't got round to it yet. On the sofa, she leans against him. He puts his arm awkwardly round her – *is this what she wants?* He can feel the blood to his arm being cut off. He tries to relax. She plays with his other hand as if his fingers were piano keys. *What does she expect of him?* Pins and needles are forming in his arm, as if his blood was crystallising. He doesn't have a free hand or he'd touch her hair or her cheek, test the water for a kiss. Her fingers are small and soft, darker than his own. She turns his hand over, and examines his palm tracing the creases with her thumb. She takes the lid off the pen and writes *palm* in his palm. The pen tickles. She blows the ink dry, her breath warm and smelling of coffee. His groin stirs. She runs her thumb over the ball of his hand. Her stroke is numbing, hypnotising. She inches her fingers under his sleeve, pushing it back to expose his wrist. His erection pushes against his trousers, a blind man looking for an exit. She writes *wrist* on his wrist. Leaning over him, she balances her mug on the arm of the sofa and moves until she sits astride his legs. Her thighs pin the cloth of his trousers against him. The blind man noses more insistently against his fly. She still holds the pen. She pulls at his T-shirt, tries to take it off. It gets stuck. He holds up his arms as if in surrender, she eases it over his head. Her clothing brushes against his bare chest. The fine hairs on his body stand alert. She leans down to kiss his neck where it meets his shoulder; but instead of kissing she writes. He can smell the ink, feel the cool drag of the pen on his skin. She bends down further and her lips graze his nipple; she writes *nipple* on his chest and then lower down, *belly button*. Her English is perfect.

*

It is popularly believed that most men think about sex every six minutes whilst women may only think about it once a day. This has helped perpetuate the idea that either women are the innocent sex or they are frigid. This in turn has licensed men over the years to behave promiscuously and to rape; men have assumed an entitlement, on the basis of the frequency of their urges, to seek out satisfaction where they can find it and to take it where it is not freely given.

As a general rule it is true that a woman's sexual desire is different in-kind from that of a man. Why not, when so much else between the sexes is different? But a mistake of the past is to make assumptions about winners and losers. Why should difference alone confer superiority on one over the other?

*

He met Chloe a month ago, during his last night in Den Bosch. There had been a party in the squat where he stayed. Any excuse. Drink, the thought of returning home, the dope. Everything melted that night. Both sad and glad to be going, he hugged everyone. He'd seen her before, but felt intimidated. She was older and French, an artist too. In the dim light the gloss of her lipstick emphasised the outward curve of her mouth, like the sticky petals that extend from carnivorous flowers; her hair was coiled and densely black. When she spoke English, her accent was a precision tool, not like the Om Pah Pah of Dutch he'd become used to. Most of the others in the squat were into green politics, or worked with refugees or people in drug rehabilitation programmes. He felt embarrassed for being an artist. At first he had been in awe of his hosts and their country; they were slim and blond, as tall as sunflowers, inhabitants of a paradise of fresh air, bicycles and comfortable clothes. Towards the end he looked forward to returning home. He wanted to see a hill again, to see a bit of countryside that didn't have a prescribed use, that wasn't under plastic or taken up with growing artificially fat tomatoes.

The morning after the party she'd driven him to Schipol airport in her draughty 2CV. A month later, he stood at the airport in Edinburgh in front of the arrival/departure panels, waiting for her plane to land. The two airports neatly bracketed the time that they had spent apart.

*

Sexual attractiveness comes high on the list of desirable attributes. Unlike 'intelligence' it connects directly to our basic instincts, bypassing however many hundreds of years of civilisation, taking us right back to the hierarchies of the tribe. Consumer culture taps the resultant anxiety like a mosquito drawing blood from the body of its host. You will spend more than you can afford in order to increase your sexual attractiveness. Your life is a sine curve defined by the peak and trough of your reproductive capability. Your sexual attractiveness is the marketing which determines your exchange value.

*

The arrivals panel flashed: Chloe's flight was delayed.

His memory of Holland is coloured by the day that he cycled along the canal and through the woods to a Nazi detention centre. There were no signposts. Only walls remained, dividing up the ground with the outline of buildings. It was February. The trees had no leaves; knuckled branches grasped at a sky that looked as if it had been rubbed out. There were no birds, no noise, except for the snap of twigs, brittle as old bones, under his feet. When he left, a force field extending out from that place seemed to follow him. Since that day, a hushed silence lay just beneath the surface of everything. Or perhaps it was just the effects of a cumulative isolation that comes from not speaking the language, the way that silence roars in your ears when you are alone. He was just a visitor. He was in Dem Bosch on a residency to make art, to paint pictures, so that's what he did. He painted space stations and satellites. Men on the moon. The others stopped making an effort. They went back to speaking Dutch in their heated discussions over the kitchen table. And then he had met Chloe.

As she was older, had a child, was a more successful artist than him, he'd thought she wouldn't be interested. He'd seen some of her work in a group show in one of the galleries. Little papermaché figures, painted and glazed, all female, doubled-over, thigh-smacking, rolling on the floor, all laughing. Each figure, the gallery hand-out had explained, was made from chewed-up bibles. She had stripped out pages, one bible at a time, as a performance piece, filling her mouth with them and chewing until the paper was reduced to a grey pulp. She had spat the pulp into jars and later moulded it into figures. *Would the inside of her mouth taste of incense and*

mildew? What did she do with the covers? The figures had names:
Sarah, Mary, Ruth...

*

Evolutionarily speaking, the worst thing a man can do is bring up
another man's child; all his energy and resources are used up in the
perpetuation of another man's genes.

*

Arrivals. The panel flashed again. His heart beat, maybe for nothing.
They had exchanged emails, light and breezy: *Hi Stephen, how's it
going...*

Batting them gently back and forth. And then they had got more
intense: *Stephen, I dreamed about you again last night...* and in
his replies he told her things he'd not told anyone before. Now
that they are going to meet again, he is not sure how they and their
email-selves will tally. Email can become detached from the sender,
like a ventriloquist's dummy, or like a hybrid of the sender and
recipient, the one's words fleshed out by the other's projections
and desires.

She must be claiming her baggage.

He didn't need the complications or the expense of a long-term
relationship. Especially not one with a child in tow – two-for-one.
He had arranged for her to give a lecture at the Art College where
he worked; eggs had been divided between more than one basket.
The College paid for a hotel too; so no assumptions needed to be
made about sleeping arrangements. He could just wait and see.

People poured out of the exit.

She was smaller than he remembered, as if she'd been cut out of
a different sized photograph from everyone else. The way she dressed
was precise, her pink coat was like something a doll might wear. He
kissed her, or bent to her kiss; who can tell who inched forward first?
A continental one-two. Hands reached out and touched each other
on the arm. Neutral territory. Establishing contact.

– How was your flight?

She nodded and smiled at him. He took her rucksack, slung it over one shoulder. She kept her hand luggage.

– We'll get a taxi.

Again she was silent.

– I thought we could go to the hotel first, drop off your things, and then if you like I'll show you around the College, before your lecture.

And that's when she did it. She smiled and took a notebook and pen out of her bag. She held the notebook under his face where he could see it. The handwriting was peculiarly French, a style that he remembered from the white boards in the language-lab at school: *Bonjour! Thankyou, yes, I had a pleasant flight.*

He stopped, reached for the notebook as if touching it would make the situation clearer. She pulled it away.

– Have you lost your voice?

She flipped over a page and, as if it were toast on a toasting fork, held it to his face again.

No, I've not lost my voice.

As a response to the war, I have decided not to speak.

She turned the page, held it up to his face as if browning the other side.

It's a performance piece. It's my protest, a response to feeling powerless.

He reached for the notebook again and the pen she was holding, but she pulled them away. *Was this a joke? Was she mad? What was the point in her being here if she chose not to speak? What about the bloody lecture? He'd gone out on a limb to get her that.*

*

In a single day a man may produce one hundred million sperm, whereas a woman between puberty and the menopause will release around four hundred eggs. It follows then that men are able to pass on their genes to far more off-spring than women. The current record for fathering children is held by one Moulay Ismail the Bloodthirsty who sired 888 children before collapsing, a spent force, at aged fifty-five in 1727. The equivalent record held by a woman goes to Madame Vassilyvev who produced 69 children, bunched conveniently in sets of twins, triplets and quadruplets, before keeling over in 1765 at the comparatively young age of forty.

What's the relevance of this? Well, the point is that the consequences of reproduction for men and women are very different. A man fulfils his biological destiny with a little rub, the stiffening of his member and the ejaculation of his seed. Point and shoot. Over in the blink of an eye. Women on the other hand, to secure the future of their genes, invest longer in the production of each child. Forty-weeks gestation, 6 months or more breastfeeding, 16 years of nurturing outside the womb.

Is it any wonder that in a recent experiment amongst university students in which men were approached by a woman unknown to them who invited them to have sex with her, three-quarters readily agreed. Women taking part in a similar experiment turned the young man down with a polite no thankyou. Okay, advances in contraception in the twentieth-century provide both sexes with a variety of options to inhibit procreation, but instinct runs deep. Instinct is not easily diverted.

*

Before Chloe arrived, a week or two in advance, he had booked a table for two, at one of the expensive seafood restaurants down by the shore. He had imagined their evening: the light fading, candles, some unobtrusive music, the murmur of conversation, a slice of sweet white fish, as firm as a well toned arm or leg, as if they were eating each other's bodies, delicately bathed in butter, herbs and garlic.

The lecture had gone well, the students had loved her. She played a video-diary consisting of a collection of freely associated thoughts about the war, recorded a few days before it began, and about her work as she went about her business, brushing her teeth, getting dressed, just going out, just coming in... She showed slides and took questions, writing the answers on a flip-chart in that curly writing of hers.

Afterwards, when they actually got to the restaurant, he felt conspicuous, as if he were dining alone or with someone with an embarrassing disability. The other tables hummed with Friday night good humour; from their table there was just the sound of his voice, cowed almost to a whisper, and the squeak, squeak of her black felt pen on paper. She pointed and he ordered for her. Her responses to his questions were curbed by the diameter of the notepad. He drank more than he'd intended, they both did. He felt stung by the bill; he'd paid and left a generous tip too, smiling, not wanting to let his shock at the cost of the evening show.

*

So you see, the point is not that women are coy, shying away from sex for fear that it should affront their delicate sensibilities. On the contrary, women, on an instinctive level, require something different from sex than men: they are after quality not quantity and with reason are keen to vet potential candidates from the disorderly queues of hopeful males who may line up to fertilise their eggs. Women are not numbed, cowed or awed. They are not merely recipients. To a large degree they control access to heterosexual sex. They are the gatekeepers of the species.

*

It's Saturday evening and he's at the airport again saying goodbye. He needn't have escorted her, except maybe she'd have found it difficult to get a cab. She hadn't stayed last night. What seemed promising had frizzled out. She had not after all wanted to sleep with him. She labelled his component parts one by one and then requested a taxi. *Bitch!* In the shower this morning he hadn't been unable to remove all the traces of the permanent marker from his body. *She'd led him on.* After she'd left last night, he'd milked himself into his t-shirt and then again that morning in the shower, but he hadn't been able to more than postpone the itch. Her perfume and the proximity of her small body stirs the dumb creature in his pants.

Au revoir!

She hands him the last page from her notebook and they kiss each other on the cheeks, a kind of undoing of the same dipping forward action of the day before. She disappears through the gate as if the film of his life is being played backwards.

66

From the top deck of the bus back to town, he watches the planes glide stiffly across the tarmac. Bleeping little trucks carrying baggage skate into position. He thinks he sees her pink jacket in the distance walking towards the plane and disappearing into the mobile walkway, but he can't be sure.

THE FLIGHT OF THE WEATHERMAN

Evan Rosenthal

THE FLIGHT OF THE WEATHERMAN

Evan Rosenthal

LEMMING CITY IS a peaceful place full of low-key, normal American folk. It is called *city*, but in reality, we are more of a large town. So when the call came with a 10-56 over at the Heaven's View, I knew it would be something out of the ordinary.

I arrived approximately thirty minutes after the event. An angry storm was raging like there'd been a tragedy up above. Sheets of furious rain plummeted down; the wind howled something fierce; lightening bolts flashed and the delayed thunderous cracks sounded like they hit inches behind you.

The Heaven's View apartment building, on Grand Boulevard, is the tallest building in the county. It stands tall next to the Olympus River, which runs past the building just down a grassy embankment. Speculators built Heaven's View back in the '60s when Lemming City was set to expand. There were going to be people moving in from all over due to a new plastic company: a corporate headquarters and a production facility. But the company went under and no one came. The city was left with one high-rise apartment building: Heaven's View, twenty floors – the tallest around by sixteen storeys.

The scene of the investigation was purportedly the penthouse suite. The top of the town, its view supposedly saw clear out to the farms. I'd never been up that high before. I couldn't imagine having my house up twenty floors from the ground. In New York City and Tokyo, they say most people live that way. Not me.

I got out of my car into the rain, which dropped down out of the sky and splashed back off the ground getting my ankles and socks wet. The river just next to the building was creeping up the embankment, swelling with the new additions. Mac and Lewis responded to the call first and Lewis was upstairs with the only witness; Mac was poking about the river's edge with his flashlight.

'Find the body yet?' I asked him.

'Nope.'

He shined the flashlight on a spot in the grass, not far from the building. There looked to be some blood mixed in with the rain, slowly being washed away. He moved the flashlight down the embankment into the rushing water.

'Might have bounced and slid down into the drink,' he said.

'Who is it?' I asked.

'Gill Fish.'

'The weather man?'

'Yep.'

The elevator door opened right into the apartment. The top floor, where Gill Fish, the 'Lord of the Weather' lived. The interior was white as could be: the walls, carpet, even the furniture. A big couch and sectional was fluffy white, like a cloud. There were a lot of mirrors. And the place was spotlessly clean. It was night, but I've never been in a brighter room.

Lewis was with the witness: Bruce Stark's girl, Lacy. She was a senior at Central and hosted the public access television shows and was going to college next year to study broadcasting. Everyone in town knew she'd be a star some day – a modern day Marilyn Monroe. She sat on one of the couches with her hands in her lap clutching her purse. Her eye make-up was smeared down her cheek. I sat down next to her and smiled my best to make her feel comfortable.

'Lacy, your father is on his way to pick you up. But first I want to ask you some questions.'

She nodded with what looked like an exaggerated frown and blinked a couple times.

'Do you want a cup of coffee?' I asked her.

'I don't drink coffee,' she said and sniffled.

'Lewis, could you get us some coffee? I could use one, maybe Lacy will want one later.' Whenever I speak to witnesses, I like to offer them alcohol. But Lacy was under the legal age. When that happens, I offer coffee. They work the same way. It loosens their tongues and gets them talking. It also means I'm giving them a gift. And since I'm offering them something, they feel like offering me something in return. It tends to work.

'All right Lacy. Let's start from the beginning. How long have you known Mr Fish?'

'I just met him in person this morning,' she said with a sob. She took a few long breaths. I waited for her to finish before asking the next question.

'Do you mind telling me what happened today, from the beginning?'

She composed herself, then began to speak. The girl was a good talker; her public access television experience showed. Once she started, there really wasn't much need for me to ask questions. Like she was putting on a performance.

'Today was career day at school. The day when seniors get out of classes and shadow professionals in their desired career path. Well, I got to shadow Gill Fish for the entire day. I had to write him three letters and I called him every week until I got hold of him. No one's ever got to shadow Gill Fish, but I was persistent. Every one of my friends was jealous. He's the only celebrity this town has.

'Well, I arrived at the Channel Three offices at 9:00 this morning. Mr Fish wasn't there. But they let me in the real studio and I got a chance to watch the people at work. I had my notebook so I just took notes. By 9:45 Gill came in for his 10:00 forecast. It was amazing: he came gliding into the room in his white suit and that sky blue shirt and white tie. He came right up to me and stared into my face with his intense look. I didn't know what to do, I felt like a deer in headlights. He's so lovely. Then he said in his baritone voice, that German, or is it an English accent? I'm not sure where he's from, but not around here. Anyway, he said, 'Lacy. You will learn a lot today. Just watch me, take notes, and try to keep up with what's going on. Please Lacy, no questions till after the 11:00 evening show, then, we can speak, *alone*. For now, Lacy, just stay out of the way.'

'That made me even more nervous than I already was. I knew that great people did things in weird ways, and he's won all those awards, so I needed to just listen and think of questions to ask at the end of the day when I would be alone with him.

'Gill then was approached by Mary; she's the production assistant and wears a headset. She shouted to him, 'Less than fifteen minutes Gill.'

'Gill went over to his desk and looked around a bit. His face became a little frustrated and he said to me, because I was standing right there, 'Where's the Doppler readout?'

'I didn't know what he was talking about. I just shrugged. Then he yelled out, 'Where's the FUCKING Doppler readout?'

'Mary came rushing over apologizing. She handed him the sheet and whispered to me, 'Don't mind him, he's what we call an eccentric genius. Those are his ways.'

'Lacy, right?' Gill said to me, interrupting Mary. I nodded. 'Come with me. You're about to see the work of the divine.'

'He rushed through the office to the back door where there was an emergency exit. I followed him into the stairwell and up to the top. He climbed a ladder and went through a hatch onto the roof. As I climbed up, I started to say, 'Mr Fish, what...' and he shushed me.

'His massive hands covered his eyes as he stood on the roof. I never realized how large and strong his hands were – powerful and solid with big veins. He had them up over his face and he spun his body in slow circles. He lifted his hands up towards the sky with his palms out and eyes closed. For about ten minutes, he rotated ever so slowly. His face was tensed up and he looked to be concentrating very hard.

'Finally, he was done and without saying anything to me opened his eyes. I tell you, his eyes twinkled. He smiled at me, that same smile – showing his teeth – he gives when the weather is sunny.

'His 10:00 performance was brilliant. I watched him work the green board. You know the weather maps are really not on the wall, it is just a green board. There are separate TV screens on the side of the stage that show the maps that you see on TV. As a weather forecaster, you have to watch the screens and pretend it is on the green wall. Mr Fish is an expert. He barely looked at the pictures from the screens while he directed his hands on the blank green wall. It was amazing. Mary watched with me and explained everything.

'There's no one like Gill who can do the green wall with such skill.' Mary said with ritual-like seriousness. 'You can even watch the Weather Channel. Even those meteorologists there have nothing on Gill. He's also got the best accuracy rating in the state. If they kept national records, he'd probably be the best as well. You're watching genius. Lemming City is lucky to have him.'

'Mary's right. At school, of course all the girls swoon over Gill. Besides his perfect looks, he's got that great smile with those teeth – and those big hands. My Mom thinks he could be in the movies.

'When Gill finished the morning forecast he left the building without saying goodbye to me. He seemed tired out from his performance. Mary told me that he needs to replenish his energy for the next show, that he was exasperated.

'Mary let me try giving a forecast using the green wall. I worked hard watching the screen and pointing to the correct parts of the map. It takes a lot of coordination. At first, my hand placement was off almost every time and I stared at the screen too much. You're supposed to keep looking at the camera as much as possible and not show that you're looking at the screens. Like Gill. You can never tell that he looks at the screens. Mary said that sometimes, somehow she thinks he doesn't. He's that good.'

Lewis came in with the coffees. I accepted one and handed Lacy the other. Nothing seemed awry in the story and I couldn't think of any reason it would come to this point with such a successful and talented man. And his accent, I could never figure out his accent. We don't have many foreigners in Lemming, so no one spoke like him. It sounded old-fashioned. My wife once called it archaic. I think that's how people from England talk.

'Drink this,' I said.

'Her father's downstairs with Mac.' Lewis told me.

'Tell him we'll just be a few minutes. Then she's free to go.'

'Sure thing.'

Lacy ended up drinking her coffee, holding the cup with both hands. As she took a sip, I asked Mac in a whisper, 'Find a body yet?'

Mac shook his head and grimaced.

Gill Fish was a loner in our town. No one knew much about him. Besides his appearances on television, no one really had much contact with the guy. Sometimes I'd seen him dining by himself. He wasn't married and had no kids. Well, none anybody knew of. Many people thought he drove into the bigger cities to be with other famous people on the weekends.

Don't get me wrong. Gill Fish never said a harsh or stuck-up word to anyone. He might have been reserved, quiet, and to himself, but every time I met him he was genial. He did all the charity functions and gave speeches at the benefit raffles. Whenever someone asked him a favour, he'd do it. But he was never one to stay and chat afterwards.

'All right Lacy,' I said. 'Then what happened?'

'He left and I didn't see him again till the 6:00 news.'

'Well why don't you just tell me what happened when you returned.'

'I was with Mary for most of the day. She let me practise on the green board more and I was getting pretty good. Gill was expected back for his 6:00. It was getting close to time with no sight of him, but Mary told me that he always makes it. His routine is to go to the roof first, for what Mary calls his inspiration, then to the stage. He does all his make-up by himself, not that he needed much.

'At about a quarter-to he came bolting in. He looked aggravated. Mary prepared the Doppler readout and he grabbed it as he rushed to the stairwell. I hurried after him. He bounded up the stairs and I followed. As he climbed the ladder he shot a fierce look down to me and said, 'Stay down there! There's action!'

'On the forecast he swept his hand across the screen. 'I have a *storm* front coming in from the west! And it's pushing down *hard*! You're going to *feel* precipitation; you're going to *hear* thunder; you're going to *see* lightning!'

'After he was done the studio applauded. He looked spent and tired as he stumbled off the stage and walked out. But he put on a great performance.'

The thunder crackled outside. I had seen that performance from the station and remembered it well. It was spectacular. And by the looks of the night, he was dead on. I wondered why a man with such prestige, a man with such skill at his job and such a bright future would want to end it like this. Maybe he was overworked… I didn't know.

'Lacy, Did he seem to be under too much stress?'

She shrugged. 'Maybe.'

'So what happened next?'

'At the 11:00 performance he was more calm. He was serious but intense as he warned about possible flooding and rain into early the next morning. After the forecast he approached me. 'Lacy,' he said. 'Now's the time I will answer your questions, *alone*. Do you need a ride home? I can drive you.'

'So instead of the bus, I got to ride in his car. You know his white old-fashioned Cadillac *Eldorado*. As I sat down, he looked at me. He used that same intense stare as when there's storms or clouds. The one he gave earlier, except directly to me. He said in an even lower tone, almost a rumble, 'Lacy, do you need to be home by any time in particular?'

'I said, 'No.'

'How would you like to come back to my apartment. It is the top of the town. You can ask me questions there, *alone*. Then I can take you home. I'd prefer that, because in my car, I listen to music. Is that all right Lacy?'

'I nodded. It was definitely all right.

'Gill then turned on the car and pulled out a CD.

'What's that?' I asked him. I wanted to know the music Gill Fish listened to.

'Wagner,' is what he said. 'Only Wagner.'

'He turned it up very loud. It was that kind of music with a loud opera choir. With big drum beats. I never imagined anyone actually listened to that kind of music, people around here only listen to country stations and rock'n'roll. I enjoyed riding in his car listening to the music. The music and being with Gill in such a fancy car made me feel powerful.

'When we reached the Heaven's View I followed him up. I couldn't believe this place. It looks like Hollywood or something – right here in Lemming City.

'Gill sat down on the couch and he looked at me very serious and said, 'Lacy, I have something very important to tell you.'

'What's that?' I responded.

'Lacy... no one's ever been to my apartment before.'

'I don't believe that.' I told him. 'You're *Gill Fish*. You must have so many famous friends.'

'He shook his head with his mouth closed. 'It's lonely up here... at the top,' he said. 'When you're up above looking down on everyone. Just me up here in the clouds.'

'Who would have thought *him* to be lonely?

'Do *you* get lonely down there?' he asked me.

'No,' I said. 'I have my boyfriend Billy-Bob Stanton. He plays on the football team and we're going to the same college next year.'

'At that, Mr Fish stood up and began pacing the room. His mood changed like when a storm cloud suddenly blows in front of the sun. I never thought he'd tell me he was lonely. I think it made him embarrassed, but I just wanted to ask him questions.

'Can I ask you my questions now?' I asked.

'Mr Fish opened the cupboard to his stereo.

'More Wagner. *Flight of the Valkyries*,' he said, not even answering my question.

'I liked the music and everything, but I didn't want to hear more of it. Plus, I needed to write a report on my experience. It's due Monday and I had yet to ask him any questions. We have an interview form to fill out.

'Just a few questions, Mr Fish. For my report,' I said to him.

'He pressed play and then began pacing the room. I don't know if you've ever heard the song. But it sounds like superhero music. Gill strutted around the room in his white suit with his chest out, his body tensed up. The music started soft, but it began to get more intense.

'Just a couple of questions...' I persisted, but in a nice way. 'Please...'

'ASK!' he yelled.

'I was confused and didn't really know what to do. The music was loud and for some reason he seemed angry. I stammered for a second.

'ASK YOUR QUESTIONS!' he screamed over the music.

'What made you decide to be a weather man?' I said. It was first on the list.

'I WAS *BORN* FOR THE JOB!' he yelled.

'I wrote the answer down on the line. My hand shook because the music was getting louder and more intense, and he was screaming.

'WHAT ELSE?! WHAT MORE MUST YOU ASK?' he shouted as he stomped about the room.

'I had another question on my sheet. It asked what skills he needed for the job. But I wanted to know what everyone else in town wanted to know. I couldn't help it.

'How are you so good at predicting the forecast?' I blurted out.

'WHAT?!' he said wildly. Looking at me with a powerful glance.

'HOW ARE YOU SO GOOD?' I yelled. 'HOW DO YOU KNOW THE WEATHER ALL THE TIME?'

'HOW DO I KNOW?' he shouted and raised his arms like he did earlier on the roof. He laughed a loud cackle. 'I CONTROL THE WEATHER! HOW COULD I BE WRONG?' he exclaimed and laughed louder.

'The music was playing at such a high volume we were both shouting and he wasn't making much sense.

'WHAT DO YOU MEAN?' I yelled. 'ONLY GOD CAN CONTROL THE WEATHER.'

'EXACTLY!' he screamed as he pumped his arms in pure glee. He grinned like a criminal in a movie. I was terribly confused.

'DO *YOU* THINK *YOU'RE* GOD?' I asked him.

'DO I *THINK* I'M GOD... I *AM* GOD!' He let out a primal scream.

'WHAT?!' I shouted.

'I... AM... **GOD**!' he said and bolted towards the balcony.

'Those were his last words. He opened the sliding door and

stepped out. He climbed onto the railing and stood on the banister with his arms raised up to the sky. The rain poured down onto him and the lightning flashed and I caught a glimpse of his huge hands. Then he leaned forward and in the next flash was gone. All I heard was the music. That's when I dialed 911.'

Lacy looked at me, expecting to find an answer. I've been in this business a long time, but have never heard of something this odd. But I've also been in the business long enough to know whether or not she was lying; this girl was telling the truth.

'Thanks,' I said.

'Did I do anything wrong?' she asked.

'No, you can go down to your father now. Tell him I said hello.'

She left and I stood by myself in Gill Fish's apartment. I examined the place. It was a strange living space for someone in these parts. It was unnatural being that high up. Must have gotten to him living like that, so different from everyone else. An odd man, an eccentric – that must explain it; so it seems. Who would have guessed? A case of loneliness. That's what fame and talent can do – as Gill Fish said himself, 'It's lonely at the top.'

We had the county send divers up to search the River, even miles up stream – but we never found Gill Fish's body. Maybe it works out better that way. For someone so great, it was probably best off not being with normal people like us.

THE FIRST ILLUMINATION OF LILY LEVALLE

Liz Berry

THE FIRST ILLUMINATION OF LILY LEVALLE

Liz Berry

AT THIRTY-SIX AND A HALF, Lily Levalle had her tender heart illuminated by a teenage boy; an exchange student from Hungary with the cheap transitory heart of a travelling salesman. She loved him in the frantic, guilty, electrifying way that women who work in libraries and whose inner clocks tick-tock ever louder, so often do. Her first meeting with him in the sports and leisure section was a small epiphany. His dark eyes and taut olive limbs, the stinking foreign cigarettes she imagined he smoked, his soft vowels and awkward consonants, all confirmed in her a desire to pursue him to the death, to not sleep at night until she had pushed her soft fumbling hands against his skin, made him beg for her, made him cry, marked her place in him like a page in a book.

But Lily was not a woman who pursued to the death, for this was a moment of revelation and not regularity. She was a quiet, softly spoken woman with mousy hair and hazel eyes who laughed in a high bell-like way and who held books as gently as babies. Yet the boy ignited in Lily a feeling she could not quite place but was certain she had not felt for a long long time. Audacity perhaps: that fluttering careless confidence that belonged only to pre-pubescent girls. The self-certainty that sent them clattering along pavements, bold and sulky. The confidence that let them look men straight in the eyes and carry on looking, bored and self-sure, ever-mocking, all-knowing. A confidence that girls as they grew to be women, slipped off shamefully and hid away in their cupboards with clothes too small and heels too high and dreams too big; useless and unthinkable, ridiculous in a world of endless diets and harsh shop lighting and magazine quizzes in which you diagnosed yourself undeserving to be loved.

Yet as Lily shelved books and watched the boy move she felt the dark stirrings of bravado inside her. Out of place in the library where speaking and staring was forbidden, Lily felt suddenly like a thing shocking and exotic: a bloom bright and unsettling in a January garden, a scarlet bra under a snow white school shirt.

'Excuse me. Can I help you at all?'

There it was. Her soft mousy voice hardly hers at all. The boy turned and looked at her. Her stomach lurched. He was exquisite. His eyes glassy and bright, shocking in the context of his face, hungry, wolfish. Little Red Riding Hood. Teeth and eyes and big rough hands. She pushed her fringe to one side and smiled helpfully at him. A librarian's smile.

'I'm looking for *Romeo and Juliet*,' he said. Her heart collapsed like a soufflé. 'And the timetable for the swimming baths.'

Lily again smiled at the boy and led him over to the Shakespeare section. Big dusty volumes with fake leather covers and endless pencilled annotations inside: *dramatic irony, pathetic fallacy,* '*soft, what light from yonder window breaks…*' She pulled out a copy of *Romeo and Juliet* and handed it to him, letting her fingers linger upon the spine.

'Is it for an exam?' she asked.

'Yes,' he said.

'And how old are you?'

'What?'

'How old… are you?' Lily felt a blush but steeled herself against it. Confidence, she thought, icy cold, the sort that tall thin blonde women in films exude; desirable but impenetrable, glacial control, a hard veneer of poise. She looked at the boy, straight into his wolf eyes.

'Eighteen,' he said, 'next week.'

Lily Levalle's heart lit up like fireworks. 'So young,' she said, smiling her helpful smile. 'The timetables are by the counter. Would you like me to show you?'

The boy smiled. 'Thank you.'

* * *

That night as Lily Levalle drove home her body crackled like a pylon with the thought of the boy. As she accelerated across the ringroad traffic lights on amber, she imagined the electricity running blue through her veins, sparking as it moved. She overtook people in estate cars, braked too sharply, put her foot down on bends like a woman possessed. Lily Levalle, thirty-six, with her tender heart and librarian smile, was a firework display of newly lit desire – all the more spectacular as it had arrived so late.

Once inside her empty house Lily kicked off her sensible black court shoes and let her toes wiggle gently in the soft pile of her carpet as she drank a weak gin and tonic. The house was always empty now but she preferred it like that. For eleven years she had lived with a man, a mathematics teacher, who spoke to her in algebra and turned the lights off in bed so he could not see her face. In the darkness she would lie there and imagine she was someone else. Never stopping for a moment to consider that perhaps she should be wishing that he was someone else. It was during those long mathematical years that her voice became soft and her hair mousy. Her life a subtractions sum, slowly reducing her to tiny unsolvable parts. But a year ago the mathematics teacher had left her for a sales assistant: a blonde woman with bleached white teeth and a false make-up face. The day he moved out Lily had smoked a cigarette for the first time in thirteen years, a menthol she'd been saving in case of emergency. The clean minty taste of the smoke in her throat preventing her from choking on her own pungent hatred.

But now Lily Levalle drank a weak gin and tonic and smiled in the mirror at her own pinking cheeks and hazel eyes. She thought of the boy: his eyes, his hands, the smell of his cigarettes, and delicately, Lily Levalle unfastened the first three buttons of her librarian's blouse and ran her fingers across the cupping of her white department store bra, as softly as if it were a Shakespeare or a first edition Plath. For who touched women as they grew old, thought Lily? Husbands grew bored and tired and routine. Lights were flicked off. Ridiculous outfits bought full of hope: revolting red lace and cheap black net that cut into dough thighs and made you foolish in your inadequacy. For who touched women as they grew old? Young boys of course, thought Lily Levalle, for tonight she was a human firework, with audacity in her heart and the car keys in her hand. She tidied herself up and leapt into her car, slamming the front door, and pulling quickly away, applying her lipstick in the rear view mirror as she went. As she drove she thought about all the boys she'd ever known, the disappointments: the first boy who'd ever kissed her, the first to touch her, the first who broke her tender heart. She turned the radio up louder and thought of them: the fumbles, the whispers, the soggy cheap valentines, the tears in the dark. *Baby love, my baby love...* '*How do I love thee, Let me count the ways...*'

When she reached the swimming pool, Lily could smell the Summer in the teatime air: the grass, the chlorine, the fleshy scent of barbecue in somebody's back garden. At the enquiries desk she smiled her helpful librarian smile and bought a spectator's ticket for the swimming pool. Sitting up in the bleachers, she gently inhaled the cleanliness into her lungs, waiting. She watched little girls floating white and tender as lilies on the water, their arm bands holding them as still as her own reflection, Narcissus in the pool, sighing with a lover's longing for all that she had lost.

After an hour and a half the boy finally appeared as Lily began to fade. Yet the sight of him semi-naked, sent a current through her body she feared might electrocute the pool. He slipped into the water with amphibian ease and swam and swam, Lily watching him with her fingers fluttering against her unruly heart. For forty-five minutes the boy swam; his limbs exotic and strong in the water, his breath gasping as he came up for air. Finally, he pulled himself out of the water and shook like a puppy before padding off to dress. Lily leapt up. Glacial, she told herself, poise, control. She went outside and lit a cigarette, waiting by the doors, her heart thumping and her gut lurching.

She saw him coming before he saw her. She smiled, ready.

'Hello,' she said, trying to look casual.

He looked at her, blank.

'How's *Romeo and Juliet*?'

'Oh!' he said. 'I'm sorry, I didn't...'

'It's all right,' said Lily.

'Yes' he said. It was a little awkward now.

'So are you here on holiday?'

'No,' he said, 'I'm a student, on exchange. From Hungary.'

'Hungary?' Lily breathed and took a deep drag on her cigarette. 'Would you like to come home with me?'

There was a silence, heavy and sinking in the pit of Lily's stomach. 'Pardon?'

'Would you perhaps like to come home with me?'

'I'm sorry, I don't...'

Lily put out her cigarette and looked at him. Looked at him in a way she used to look at boys. *Baby love, my baby love...*

'I'd like you to. Please.'

The boy looked at her, confused. What big eyes you have, she thought, what teeth, what hands. She turned and began to walk away towards her car. As she reached her door she looked up; the boy was behind her, lamb like now, expectant, a wolf in sheep's clothing.

'I don't...' he murmured.

'Neither do I' said Lily, her voice soft but her glacial veneer as smooth as a skating rink.

They got into her car and drove home. Neither spoke very much. Lily asked questions and he replied in a perfect, stilted English that made her hands clutch the wheel with a trembling grasp. When they got home Lily poured herself a strong gin and tonic and smiled at him, her knees shaking a little.

'So, *Romeo and Juliet*...' she said, teacherish, awkward.

He looked at her. 'Would you like to go upstairs.'

'Yes,' said Lily. 'Yes I would.'

So Lily Levalle, thirty-six, was led upstairs by the Hungarian exchange with wolfish eyes and the cheap transitory heart of a travelling salesman. Never before had it been like this. As she pressed herself close against him and let him undress her, her lungs were filled with the scent of his cigarettes and clean smell of chlorine. There were no equations, no algebraic language, no darkness. Just intoxication. As he kissed her, Lily Levalle felt the tight ribbons of her bitter, slivered heart unravel and uncurl in a maypole dance. She imagined butterflies exploding from cocoons inside her, tiny birds, ladybirds, starfish, goldfish. Her head swam. She clutched onto him, desperate in a way she had never been before, pressed into the darkness, every nerve in her skin flipped on a light switch.

And in the aftermath they talked. Not pillow talk, politeness and clichés and things you didn't mean, his English and inexperience wouldn't allow for that. But real talk. She told him about the library and her heartache and the mathematics teacher and his sales assistant. About the things she wanted and the things she had lost, the confessions she whispered into the darkness at night. He talked about Hungary and his family and why he liked to swim. And as Lily Levalle went to sleep that night, her fingers clutching at the Hungarian exchange whose name was Stefan and who was only seventeen, she felt her body at last light up as it had promised to do for so many years in that mathematical wilderness.

And in the morning when her bed was empty and the Hungarian gone, slipped out, wolfish in the bird song of dawn, Lily Levalle lay quietly in bed. Star-crossed. There was a smell of closeness in the room, cloying and sticky. She got up. He will not be back, she thought, pulling open her curtains, but still she smouldered and in the harsh glare of daylight did not fade to black. Miss Lily Levalle smiled at herself with a librarian's smile, drenching the street in the light of her illumination. *Baby love,* she mouthed, bright as a star, *'soft what light from yonder window breaks…'*

SOMETHING'S COMING

Amanda Robinson

SOMETHING'S COMING

Amanda Robinson

HELEN PREPARED A SMILE as she rang the doorbell. Lately her married female friends had started behaving as if she was a cheetah skulking about in the long grass, waiting to pick off their husbands should any of them stray too far from the herd. As if she wanted any of their poxy husbands anyway. (Well there were one or two.) These days it seemed whenever she arrived at one of their parties, there would always be a potential suitor planted among the guests. Helen's favourite game was to guess who it was before he was served up to her in a typically casual manner that utterly failed to conceal her friends' aspiring matchmaking.

Nicole's husband Des helped her out of her coat. Seeing Nicole hovering in the background, Helen applied her kiss of greeting to Des's cheek a little longer than strictly necessary, resting her fingertips on his stomach, just above his waistband. Nicole quickly darted between them, blotting Helen's lipstick from her husband's cheek, embracing Helen in a manner bordering on aggressive. Helen proffered her plastic bag.

'All the wine in your corner shop looked filthy, so I got gin.'

'Oh gin,' cooed Nicole through slightly bared teeth, 'how lovely. Des, why don't you put this in the kitchen.'

'Will do. What can I get you, Helen?'

'Er, something with gin in, please.'

'Orange juice okay? I don't think we've got any tonic.'

'Perfect,' purred Helen.

'Think I might join you in one actually,' said Des jauntily.

'Now sweetie,' admonished Nicole.

'Just a little one darling.' He patted his wife's arse in a placatory fashion before disappearing into the kitchen.

'Why don't you come through?' said Nicole. Why don't I come

through? mocked Helen in her head. Nicole, I knew you when you lived in a bedsit. You had no through to come to. Helen paused at the living room door to play her game: was it the dishy lawyer she knew vaguely? No, that bitch who was something high-up in a magazine had a proprietary claw on his arm. The gangly bloke laughing in honking great snorts? The balding fellow stuffed into tight Diesel jeans? But no, Nicole had pounced on a great bear of a man and was leading her quarry back to Helen. He wore glasses and a suit and had removed his tie, releasing a thatch of dark fur from the collar of his shirt. Christ, thought Helen, don't I at least get a drink first?

'Helen, you should meet Randy. You both like music...' before drifting off to attend to her other guests.

'Is that right?' Randy said, 'isn't it great how much stuff is on here?' American, though if she'd thought about it the name Randy would have flagged that up before he'd even opened his mouth. 'So what's the last musical you saw?'

Music*als*, Nicole, music*als*, she thought, you forgot that all-important final syllable. Helen had seen a musical, years ago, when she'd first come down to London. It was called *She Loves Me* and was now forgotten but for the fact that the two (now-divorced) stars had fallen in love and gotten married while appearing in it. Helen had bought standby tickets with a friend and thrillingly, just as the lights went down, Jack Nicholson and an entourage including his secret English child had been ushered into the seats next to them. She didn't remember much about the show, though a few days later she'd seen a poster tagged with a review plugging it as 'The Best Musical in London' and thought, well thank God I don't have to see any of the others. These days her tastes ran more to indie gigs in sweaty pub back rooms.

'Oh, well, I'm not really into musicals,' she replied. She would come to realize retrospectively that this was her big mistake. To a zealot that made her ripe for conversion, like saying, 'mmm, I'm not really sure if I believe in God' to one of those Christians who accost you in the street.

'Yeah,' he said, 'I guess there're some pretty bad ones out

there. Like I thought *Chicago* was kind of overrated. There's a revival of *West Side Story* just opened though, it's supposed to be amazing. They've stayed really faithful to Robbins' original staging.'

'Oh really?' she smiled politely. Des appeared with Helen's drink and stopped to chat to Randy. Helen snatched Nicole's arm as she passed and hissed in her ear, 'Is he actually straight?' Nicole smiled as if she'd made a great joke and glided by without answering.

Naturally they were seated next to each other at dinner. Once she had steered him away from musicals, they managed to have quite a pleasant conversation. He worked at Des's bank, recently transferred from the New York office. He started to describe what he did but was astute enough to note Helen's eyes glazing over with incomprehension and asked what she did. She tarted up her job at an obscure museum to make it sound more interesting and was surprised to learn that he'd visited there.

'Really?' she said, 'the Museum of the History of Forensic Science is not usually first on the list for newcomers to London.'

'Well, my mother is a pathologist. I really wanted to be able to send her a postcard from there.'

'Oh right. So did you actually get any further than the gift shop?'

'Sorry,' he said, pinching the bridge of his nose in distress at his gaffe, 'that came out wrong. I did really want to see it, it's a great little museum. Some of those photos are so gruesome though. Even though they're all grainy and black and white.'

'Yeah, well back in Victorian times they hadn't worked out how to mount a camera over an examining table. They had to sort of peg the bodies to the wall to photograph them.'

'So that's why some of them look so... strangulated.'

'Yes. Well that and some of them were strangled.'

By the time pudding arrived they'd discovered a mutual interest in 1930s ceramics (her unanswered question to Nicole needled briefly but was swiftly quashed) and before she knew it she'd offered to show him a couple of places in the East End that dealt in them. As they gathered their coats they arranged to meet up the following afternoon, Helen doing her best to ignore Des and Nicole regarding them smugly, like proud parents.

The next morning Helen awoke with a headache and a mouth like shoe leather. She did her habitual quick rundown of the previous evening to inspect it for any offences caused or embarrassments suffered and finding none, felt rather pleased. On the nightstand her mobile, set to vibrate, started dancing about. Randy, oh yes, there was that. She gargled a mouthful of water and answered in the most mellifluous tones she could muster.

'Hello?'

'Sorry, were you asleep?'

'No, of course not. How are you?'

'Okay. Listen, I know this is a bit presumptuous, but I've arranged something for tonight I think you'll really like. Are you free? Please say you're free.'

Helen toyed with not being free in order to seem more attractively unavailable but he sounded so entreating (and unattractively available); she didn't have the heart.

'As it happens, I am. What did you have in mind?'

'I'm going to surprise you.'

'That's so unfair. How will I know what to wear?'

'Whatever you're wearing this afternoon'll be fine.'

This did not bode well; it ruled out any swanky restaurants or nightclubs. She said goodbye and dragged herself from bed to inspect her wardrobe. Truth be told, her usual garb for trawling around antique shops was jeans and a fleece. Maybe we really are going to Pharmacy or somewhere, she thought. Maybe he thinks I go about in rich bitch gear on weekends. She selected some cream trousers that had cost her a week's salary and a cardigan around her shoulders, and pushed back her hair with some knock-off designer sunglasses. Day to evening, she thought, inspecting her reflection, perfect.

The jeans and jumper he was wearing when they met up punctured her theory somewhat. They were also not an improvement on last night's suit, emphasising his gut and slight stoop. She smiled brightly and presented her cheek for a kiss, and was rewarded with a crushing hug. He was keyed up like a small child in anticipation of the evening's entertainment, but he still wouldn't tell her what it was. Perhaps it was a jazz club, they were pretty casual and she was sure he'd mentioned jazz the night before. He relaxed when they got to the shops and started admiring vases and tea sets, sniggering at the more garish examples.

'I got a Chameleon ware vase of my grandmother's because everyone else thought it was totally cheesy,' he said. 'I didn't know anything about this stuff then, but I started seeing other pieces around and got into it. Now my brother and sister have found out it's kind of valuable and are hollering that I tricked them into letting me have it.'

'That's silly. I don't see how people can live with things they don't like, if they just think they're an investment.'

He chuckled. 'You know we have a whole department at the bank for people who do exactly that.'

Helen drifted over towards the furniture. There was a funny low dressing table panelled with mirrors. Randy's reflection joined hers in its multiple surfaces.

'I'm not so into the furniture,' he said.

'No? I like it. I like its sort of... brittle glamour.'

'Brittle glamour,' he said thoughtfully, 'that's a good phrase for...'

'For what?'

'Nothing.' He seemed embarrassed and abruptly left her side to inspect something on the other side of the shop.

Afterwards they headed back into the West End. He was agitated again, checking his watch repeatedly.

'We don't really have time to eat before... d'you know a good place around here for coffee?'

Not that I go to after six o'clock in the evening, she thought. What is it with Americans and their deviant aversion to booze? I could murder a cocktail.

They found a café and Helen made do with a tea while Randy drank some vile syrup and whipped cream confection that left froth all over his upper lip. When the stuff made it onto the tip of his nose Helen felt compelled to reach over with her napkin and sort him out but he was covered in it again with the next sip. Helen decided that if they went out again she was going to have to start carrying a hip flask. Finally Randy deemed it time to go and they walked up into Soho. They turned a corner and he made a ta-da! gesture as an illuminated theatre marquee swung into view.

'Oh! *West Side Story*! Great!'

'Have you seen it before?' he beamed.

'I think I saw the film once…'

'Oh you'll notice some differences then; they switched a few of the songs around and invented the character Ice for the movie. You know this was Sondheim's first musical? Though of course he only wrote the lyrics…'

She tuned him out as he put an arm around her and led her into the theatre. The seats were nearly in the front row. Helen wondered how much they'd cost; how many pints that would buy at her favourite grotty blues bar. Randy bought her a programme (but not a drink) and the orchestra started the intro, a medley of all the songs from the show.

Helen tried not to think of all the places that she'd rather be as she watched thirty-five year-old English men and women fling themselves about pretending to be Hispanic teenagers. Almost anywhere within a 100 yard radius. And that included some pretty dodgy peep shows and strip bars. She purposely avoided looking at Randy but when the interval came she had to face him. He was enraptured. He sat staring at the fire curtain for some moments before turning to her.

'Well? Isn't it great? I knew you'd love it.'

His self-answering question relieving her of the necessity to lie she stood up determined to hit the bar hard.

'I've gotta run to the bathroom,' he said.

'Great! I'll get the drinks. What would you like?'

'I'll just have one of those little ice creams, I love those.'

He went in search of the Men's while Helen ruthlessly tackled her way to the front of the smoky bar.

'A quadruple gin and tonic please. And one of those little ice-creams.' When the drink came she knocked back half the gin neat before topping the rest up with tonic. She turned to find Randy behind her.

'Jeez you must be thirsty,' he said.

'Yeah,' she replied, 'Here's your icecream.'

As they settled in their seats Helen consoled herself that the second halves of plays were usually shorter than the first but as the show progressed it did not feel that way. Her interval refreshment swilling through her veins, she had to bite her lip to keep from sniggering when Tony bit the dust. When it finished Randy gave the actors a (solitary) standing ovation. Helen turned to him and then looked quickly away, deeply disturbed by what appeared to be tears in his eyes.

As they walked through the streets he was on a high, alternately reliving his favourite parts and singing snatches of the songs. Helen did her best to ignore people staring as he belted out the opening to the Jet song before executing a surprisingly graceful spinning leap.

It being a Saturday night in Soho, the restaurants were jammed and they wound up in a desperate Mexican place, sandwiched between three separate shrieking hen parties. After one margarita Helen managed to slop guacamole on the priceless trousers. After four more and a limp enchilada she discovered she didn't mind any more.

'I guess girls do this in the States,' Randy was gesturing at the hen girls, 'I mean my sister had a bridal shower. But I don't think it was quite like this.'

'No? Howsit different?'

'Well for one thing a bridal shower's more like a tea party.'

Helen snorted.

'And they don't have all this... get-up. I mean that girl' – he gestured the next table, where two of the bride's companions were goading her to snog the waiter so they could tick a checklist printed on the back of her T-shirt – 'has on a plastic ball and chain, handcuffs, a veil, a temporary tattoo, at least I hope it's temporary –'

'Yeah, otherwise she might really regret her choice of a penis with devil horns on it in later life.'

'– and that L-sign, what's that?'

'It's an L-plate, like for when you're learning to...' having temporarily forgotten the word for conducting an automotive vehicle, Helen twisted her hands in front of her in a steering motion. The bride teetered and then ducked her head under the table to be sick. Her friends cheered and ticked the puking box on her shirt.

'In this country a hen night is not considered a success unless the bride is admitted to hospital with severe alcohol poisoning,' proclaimed Helen.

'Shall we go?' said Randy.

The street outside was quiet by comparison. They walked in silence, stopping to inspect the occasional darkened shop window.

'You don't really need these anymore,' said Randy, removing Helen's sunglasses from where they were still propped on top of her head.

'Help, I'm blind!' she giggled. He drew her towards him and gave her an assured kiss. She responded, snaking her arm into the small of his back. He leaned back and brushed the hair from her face.

'Would you like to come round? For coffee?' he asked.

'That would be nice,' she said. Miraculously they found a cab and were soon deposited outside his building in the lower reaches of Hampstead. Helen stared enviously up at the elaborate gothic brick facade. Up in the flat he really did make coffee. It was a small place but had uninterrupted views down into the centre of town. The anonymous furnishings must have come with it, and he didn't seem to have been there long enough to stamp his personality on it in any way. It was scrupulously neat, prompting Helen to wonder if he'd planned to ask her back or was just really anally retentive.

He emerged from the kitchen with the coffee and started fiddling with the stereo.

'What do you feel like listening to? Shall we listen to *West Side Story*?'

'Well, you know, I don't –'

'No you're right, we don't want to taint our memory of tonight's performance. A little Rogers and Hammerstein?'

It was time to come clean. 'Look, Randy. I had a lovely time tonight, it was great – thank you – but really, musicals are just not my thing.'

'But you like Sondheim, right?' he said, brandishing a CD. 'Everyone likes Sondheim.'

Helen smiled wanly and he put it on, filling the room with its atonal refrains.

He lit a candle on the coffee table (I really must ring Nicole and clear up this gay question, thought Helen) and dimmed the lights before joining her on the sofa. Helen sipped her coffee demurely for a minute before thinking, oh fuck it, and flung herself at him.

They writhed together on the sofa like teenagers for some time. Helen felt as if her whole head was coated in spit but it wasn't an entirely unpleasant sensation. With a faint whirr, the CD ended. She breathed an inward sigh of relief until Randy made as if to get up and change it. Desperately she scrabbled at the fly of his trousers, yanking them down and proceeded to give him a blow job. When she perceived the moment of musical danger to be past, she stopped and looked up at him. He was gazing at the ceiling, his hands hovering just over her head, itching to take it and guide her stroke. Noticing she'd stopped he looked down.

'Jeez. Wow. Thanks.'

'Shall we go next door?' she said.

'Yeah!'

In the bedroom they undressed without ceremony. He was much hairier than she usually liked, but in a pleasingly uniform way. He heaved his ponderous bulk over her and came almost at once. Helen wondered if he was trying to mould an impression of her into the mattress as he remained on top of her, catching his breath. She wriggled about to remind him to get off and he rolled to one side, encircling her with a well-furred arm. Before she drifted off to sleep, Helen was struck by the curious conviction that she was safe from anything while she lay under the protection of that massive paw.

She awoke a few hours later to a pungent sweet smell. Randy was snoring thunderously. She drew a blanket around herself and wandered back into the living room, where the air was thick with the scent of the still burning candle. Vanilla scented! Gadzooks! She blew it out and returned to the bedroom. After a few unsuccessful attempts at getting Randy to stop snoring she gave up and went back into the living room, curling up on the couch.

He was still asleep when she went back into the bedroom the following morning, and mercifully silent. She considered slipping back into bed with him, but the temptation of several more hours of unadulterated sleep in her own bed was too great and she quietly started gathering her clothes. He woke up and asked a little petulantly if she was going. She ruffled his hair and gave him a kiss, claiming pressing errands and chores at home.

'I'll call you,' he called after her as she left.

'So? How'd it go?' Nicole could not conceal a tone of vicarious thrill. 'Isn't Randy a sweetie?'

'Um –' stalled Helen, kicking the door to her office shut.

'Anyway you can tell me all about it tonight. Des managed to snag a table at that new Japanese place off Tottenham Court Road. Are you free?'

'I –'

'Of course you are. See you at eight.'

The restaurant was packed. Helen picked her way between tables until frantic waving from one of the cramped booths attracted her attention and she spied Des, Nicole and – her heart sank – Randy. She smiled bravely and shoehorned herself in next to him.

'I tried to call you,' he said.

'Oh I lost my phone,' Helen replied. The disloyal item started ringing deep inside her handbag. She snatched it out and switched it off.

'I, er, found it this afternoon,' she said with a hollow laugh. She sought refuge behind a menu only to recoil at the prices. Who was paying? Would it be totally cold-blooded to expect Randy to pay for her meal and then give him the heave-ho?

'We've ordered the tasting selection,' said Nicole, snatching the menu away from her. A succession of tiny, beautifully presented but unfulfilling tid-bits arrived without warning or explanation. Despite sitting almost on top of Randy, Helen couldn't have more than the most superficial conversation with him under the surveillance of Des and Nicole's manic grins. She felt like a vivisection animal at the mercy of two mad scientists. Presently Nicole excused herself and reading the barely perceptible beckoning in the tilt of her jaw, Helen followed.

As soon as they were out of earshot of the table she grabbed Nicole's arm.

'You didn't say anything about him coming along!'

'Didn't I?' said Nicole airily.

They trailed all the way down to the basement until they found a door with a picture of a Japanese woman on it. After emerging from the stalls they rinsed their hands in a long trough with a waterfall running into it that served as a sink.

'Anyway I thought you'd want to see him again,' said Nicole, 'it sounds like things went rather... well on Saturday.'

'What did he say?'

Nicole gave an enigmatic smile in reply.

'He took me to see *West Side Story*.'

Nicole let out a shriek of hilarity tinged with schadenfreude.

'It was awful. Like watching the school play performed by people old enough to know better. And I couldn't *say* anything. He loved it! He had *tears* in his eyes, I swear.'

Nicole nudged her in the ribs. 'And after?'

'After what?'

'Was he any good in the, ah, sheet department?'

'The sheet department? What, are you not allowed to say fuck after you get married? Look, he's a nice enough bloke but this isn't going anywhere. I mean *musicals*! What were you thinking?'

Nicole flinched at this affront to her matchmaking skills. 'Well I think you're being just a bit picky. You're not getting any younger you know. Randy may be a nerd –'

'Would you go out with him?'

'Don't be silly, I've got Des.'

Helen considered revealing that Des would pinch her bottom whenever opportunity presented itself while Nicole continued: 'Randy's a good catch. He's got a good job, nice flat... and he's new in town, so he doesn't know you've been, you know, about a bit.'

Helen was only distracted from slugging Nicole by Randy emerging from one of the cubicles.

'Randy!' exclaimed Nicole.

'What are you doing in the women's toilet?' cried Helen.

'It's unisex,' said Randy stonily. He swung the door inwards and Helen saw that the picture on it was actually some sort of lady-boy, dressed half as a man and half as a woman. She covered her mouth with her hands.

'How... modern,' breathed Nicole. Randy squared his shoulders and advanced towards her. Nicole cowered against the sink, dwarfed by his full height. Helen suddenly had a vision of Randy devouring Nicole in a single bite. In any case, Nicole scurried from the room before he had the opportunity. Randy calmly washed and dried his hands without looking at Helen. Unnerved by his silence she started to babble an apology.

'I'm just glad I didn't have to hear about my performance in the sheet department,' he said stiffly.

'Oh, it was... I wouldn't...' Helen stammered and gulped for air.

'Look it was partly my fault for just dragging you along without telling you what it was. But you could have told me you didn't like it. I could've taken it you know. D'you imagine I've never taken any flack, a straight guy who likes musicals?'

'I'm sorry. I just didn't want to seem ungrateful.'

He was silent. Then he started to chuckle.

'What?'

'That Nicole is a shitty matchmaker.'

Helen could not suppress a smile. 'Yeah, the musical nerd and the aging been-about-a-bit girl, what was she thinking?'

'D'you want to get out of here?' he said.

'There's a real dive of a blues bar near here,' she replied, 'the stage is the size of a postage stamp and the beer makes your kidneys ache.'

'Sounds great.'

He offered her his hand and she followed him up the stairs. She thought she could hear him humming 'Tonight' from *West Side Story* under his breath. But she couldn't be sure.

BRAGA

Suhayl Saadi

BRAGA

Suhayl Saadi

*To the fin-folk, who never disappeared, except beneath
the skin*

THE OLD RECTORY had been haunted since before it had been built.
Everyone on Brusa knew this, and most people on the islands
nearby knew it too. They had heard the stories at mother's knee,
warning them to keep away, or threatening them with some dark
figure drawn inevitably from the echoing, unvisited (yet in another
sense, much-visited) halls of Brusa Rectory. It was what had
drawn Frame to this place, after all. The incipience of a darkness,
greater than his own. He'd researched the whole matter painstak-
ingly, over half-pints of thick, dark beer and elegant, thin cigars.
He sat, alone in the summer's late evening light which slanted in
through the large latticed window, in what once had been the
Rectory library and went over it all in his mind. From outside the
window the sound of the sea came and went like breath.

For years, stretching back beyond even the long tongues of the
spey-wives, pounding Neolithic forces had danced around the flat
knoll by the water, bringing down rain or snow or wind or whatever necromantic element had been needed to fulfil their mega-
lithic, tribal rituals. Later, various axe-blooded Norsemen were
said to have used the area as unhallowed burial ground for hooded
heretics. In the sixteenth century, some stragglers from the Great
Armada of El Rey Filipo II had been shipwrecked in the cauldron
seas which rose up against the rocky coves, and had come ashore
and set up camp on the knoll. They stayed there for six nights, but
on the seventh, a great wind blew up (started, some say, by the fin-
wives of the deep who had wanted to keep the sailors for themselves) and the entire camp was swept over the edge of the cliffs.

At first it had seemed strange to Frame that a religious building would have been constructed on the site of so much unwanted psychical activity, but there it was. Perhaps, he'd hypothesised as he'd driven through the midsummer's afternoon towards the place, it had been a deliberate act on the part of the old Church custodians. A statement, if you like. In the late nineteenth century, science – even in church circles – had been in the ascendant, and the man who became the first Rector of Brusa, the Reverend Archibald Farquharson, was a Fifer who, quite simply, did not believe in ghosts. In the name of progress he'd wanted to abolish superstition once and for all from the Orkney islands, so that, by the dawn of the Electric Century, they would no longer be, as it were, islands. It was he who had driven the church to raise a respectable rectory on Brusa, that he might cater better for the growing population of the island, which had been newly-swelled by an influx of herring fishermen and their families. Frame had searched long and hard for a photograph of the man, but as yet had failed to find even one. That too seemed odd. Surely, he'd thought, such a prominent local figure in the late nineteenth and early twen-tieth centuries would have had at least one sitting before the old, static, black camera. The only solid piece of evidence relating to Rector Farquarson's existence was a one-line document which had been copied down in copperplate by some assiduous clerk from a burned fragment of a diary after the rest had been destroyed:

At midnight, the sea came to my door.

But then he'd learned from a former shepherd, an old man known on account of his once-ruddy hair as Red Hector, that after he'd died all the Rector's belongings, including a pile of books which had stretched halfway to the sky, had been burned and the ashes scattered across the waves. Not his body though. That had never been found.

Frame shuddered, and instinctively he glanced back at the equipment; an atomic chronosphere and a lenticular stereoscope;

both of which he'd placed on a broad, sturdy-legged, wooden table. The first was to measure relative time, since paranomal beings tended to exist in a variety of time-space continua which possessed quite different physical laws from those of own. The stereoscope was a fairly conventional instrument which could take several photographs at once and fuse them into a single, multi-dimensional image. The number of potential dimensions in the known universe had reached eleven, so it followed that the number in those cosmological regions which had not yet been exposed to the glare of theoretical physics eventually would attain almost Kabbalistical levels. The Victorian table and an old-fashioned desk with lots of tiny drawers were the only loose furniture left in the library, apart from two armchairs whose upholsteries, which once had been a deep gold, looked as though they had been battered by eighty years of northerly gales. And then, at the far end of the room, directly opposite the long windows, was a preacher's lectern. He tried each of them in turn and finally, sat on the one whose springs seemed a little less sprung.

The heat of the day was beginning to dissipate, yet the sky remained cloudless. The Rectory had not been visible from the road, being hidden by a clump of trees and by the rounded shoulder of the knoll's inland edge. Frame had parked his clapped-out, rusting hulk of a hatch-back just off the only road on the island, which itself, was little more than a track. Anywhere except Brusa, it would've been a track. The Ordnance Survey maps had it down as a dotted line. The Rectory itself was missing from the charts. It was as though even the ink of its existence had faded, so that now it lay unrecognised in the cartograph of this world, yet very much alive in the minds of the Brusi, as the folk of this most remote of the Orkney islands were known. Frame had pulled the car to a halt at the end of the track. The old metal chassis had creaked as, at once, it had begun to cool. He had thought of leaving the window open, but then had decided against it, and had rolled it up instead. Frame remembered thinking that the car wouldn't last long in the grey and salt of the Northern Isles. There were no vintage vehicles up here; the rust had set in, long ago.

He had been here before some days earlier when he had come to reconnoitre the area. No particular atmosphere had struck him on that occasion, but then, he had not been about to spend the night in the place. Sometimes, Frame wondered why he did this work for the Society. It was hardly fun, being treated either as a crank or an interloper. He had expected the Rectory to smell musty, dead, but actually he had found that it smelled of the sea. The water's edge lay less than 100 yards away, just a black selkie-leap from the gale-blown, latticed glass of the front window. For the Rectory had been built to face the open ocean, as though Farquharson had constructed it as a Babel to the might of the sea. As though he had challenged the sea to render up its secrets so that he might do battle on behalf of his rational, missionary god, on the sands and grasses of Brusa. Tonight though there was no breeze and the heat lay like kirkyard earth over everything. Frame was sweating from carrying in the equipment. Over the past few months he had felt a certain weakness begin to creep over his limbs. Maybe it was time to move on, to do something else, to stop searching in dark corners for that which did not exist (or which, if it did, had no desire to reveal itself). But move on where? He had come to the end of the land – beyond the end actually – because, really, where else might an extreme situation present itself? Change came only through such extremes. Once he'd had love, then he'd had none; once he'd had money, then he'd been poor. He'd been young and now... he wasn't exactly old, but time seemed to be in a state of perpetual acceleration and like a stupid fish he was caught at its centre. Well, this was his way of stepping right out of it. For a while, at least. Thinking, and writing, about paranormal phenomena rendered to his mind a place to roam, free of lawyers, money-worries, morality. There was no morality in science, and none in buildings either, if the truth be told. It was human beings who imposed moralities and Frame had had his fill of human beings and their concepts. He just wanted facts, or non-facts, it didn't matter which, really. Either way, they would lift him out of himself, and out of the darkness which lay at his centre and which made lunatic time reel ever faster onwards.

The library was empty, in fact the whole house was virtually a shell. Where books once had sat the rows of bookshelves were marked, shadowed, so that he was able to make out what the exact sizes of the volumes had been. But I'll never discover what was in the books he thought, nor what drove the good people of Brusa to pile them high and set them alight. The chronograph lay still, its needle poised above the paper at the zero mark. The stereosphere made no sound. On one occasion, some years ago, both machines had gone completely crazy, their mechanism had become possessed by what Frame – then at the beginning of his investigative career – had imagined to be some form of visitation from the other side, some kind of invisible, ectoplasmic activity, but which had turned out to be simply the raging of an underwater stream. He'd felt a fool, and had vowed never to repeat the mistake of giving in to fear. Ever since then he had investigated sites – usually houses, but sometimes open spaces – with an exactitude of which any forensic cop would've been proud. He'd been all over the British Isles, but it was the first time he'd come this far north, to this strange land which seemed to consist disproportionately of sky and water. He'd been here a week, and in spite of his long-held, rigorous, para-scientific attitude, Frame had found himself beginning to sink, mentally, into what he could only describe as sand, the white money dust of the coastline. That was why, finally, he'd decided to terminate his researches which had taken him to the incongruously pink Cathedral of Magnus with its skull'd, Masonic tombs and its perfect acoustic luminescence, into the various public libraries and into the cottages of some of the older folk of the island, and eventually, to venture into the shell of the Rectory itself.

It was said by some – Red Hector being one – that Rector Farquharson had had no wife because he'd lost her with child awhile back, and that was why, if truth be told, he'd wanted to build his house so close to the sea's edge and on a reputedly haunted site, to boot. Frame had listened to Red Hector's tale, and had accepted the cigar which the old crofter had proffered, but somehow he had doubted whether the islanders would have come to that conclusion before the disappearance of the Rector. He'd seen it first from the plane: an ugly, dark block of a building, quite out-of-place on the undulating, sandy island. It had risen like a fist towards the sky and towards the tiny nine-seater plane in which he had been travelling, and for a moment, Frame had been seized by a terrible, irrational thought that the Rectory might rise like a giant hand from the sand, from the sea, the fist opening and the fingers tearing down the plane, the sky, the world. He'd kept a close eye on the altimeter until the moment when, elegantly and remarkably comfortably, the plane had touched down on the rough stones of the landing strip. His fellow-passengers had already got off at previous stops; Brusa was last, furthest out, least regarded in the archipelagic scheme of things. That was why, when he had come again to the island – apart from the fact that he'd needed his car to haul the equipment along – he had come by ferry. The sea had seemed a lesser danger, though when he'd glanced at the poster which had been pasted like a Red Madonna to the outside of the disembarkation post, warning of unpredictable tides and incipient flooding due to the inordinate lack of incline on the island, he'd not been so sure. It seemed that Brusa, like a skerry, had just risen from the sea-bed and might return there at any time. What a place to erect a stone house Frame had thought. The three-storey Rectory was taller than it was broad and had dark, elongated windows. Like everything in Orkney it was made of a tough, grey-brown sandstone which was the hardest sandstone Frame had ever rapped his knuckles across. Not that he'd been rapping for ghosts...

He lit one of the candles he had brought with him. Midnight sun was wishful thinking on Brusa. You'd have to go another few hundred leagues north, beyond the Westrays and the Whalsays and the Yells and up to the Faeroerne, to bask on a rock in that clear light. Ah, but there was only one Whalsay, he reminded himself. But then there were two of everything really, weren't there? And especially so with these islands. There were the lands you saw and could walk on – the full-breasted mountains of Hoy, the sinking sands of Sanday, and so on – and then there were the islands which you could never see, or touch, or walk upon, unless you were Jesus. Beneath all the low crofts, the fishermen's cottages, the grass of disused manses, there lay rock the colour of sand, and beneath that, the shifting, sliding, savage female body of the sea. Wherever you went it was there. He'd felt it right from the moment he'd stepped off the plane. The smell of daberlacks, the cold sweat of the open ocean, and beneath the soles of his feet the sensation of seething magnetic waters, pulling him down, down and north.

Seven beats of the oar,
To a northern beach,
Where the sand courses like molten silver through the water,
A land of prophets, of stone tablets and steel Bibles.

And anyway, how had he known all that, the names of the different islands? He shrugged, then remembered he was alone in the room. He figured he must have read it somewhere, in some archive or other. It was funny the things which caught in the nets of your mind. The candles cast long shadows across the walls and caused certain cracks and deficiencies to appear which he hadn't noticed before. Every so often the flame would bend and sputter and dance and its movement reminded him of the silken chorea of the sea of the northern reaches, in the long leagues before the water turned to ice. He rubbed his knuckles. The rock had almost broken the skin. The rock of the wall.

Suddenly, Frame wondered why he was there. Why, really, had he come to this northern place where night never fell but where the day danced like selkie foam along the edge of the horizon as it moved, imperceptibly, widdershins, from west to east? A messy London divorce, no children, the onset of a sterile middle age, a waning, subtle but inexorable, the turning to earth… a subsistence job. The dark loneliness of the city. No solitude. It was a long time since he'd had a woman. And Frame had come at length to lose any desires he might once have regarded as being as important as food say, or breath. It was odd how one could do without those things of the flesh. The Society for Psychical Research had been his refuge. A glossy, Sabbath bolt-hole for losers and obsolescent engineers. But he had gone further than most; the whole thing had begun to take over his life, to assume control, if not of his thoughts, then of his actions. It had become almost a religious process. Not that he'd minded; it was quite comforting to feel that there might be some other moving force in the midst of his personal oblivion. A kind of sublimation perhaps. Very post-modern. Very London. The new celibacy, provoked as much by a fear of intimacy, a subtle paranoia of the senses, as a fear of the slow virus, the creep of wormwood. Love and death walked the streets of the city, hand-in-hand. Life had grown too closely to resemble the Crucifixion, and he wanted no part of it. He ran his palm over the bald surface of the chronosphere. It reminded him of an unmapped world; this is what it had been like, at the beginning. *And the spirit of God moved upon the face of the waters...* Perhaps that was what had attracted him to this place; the view of the waters, first thing in the morning, was transfiguring. He'd looked it up himself. *The Haunted Sites Of The Orcades.* A blusteringly pompous, mid-twentieth century tome, long out-of-print, penned by some Middle English colonel-type for upper middle class tourists with a middling familiarity with the colonies and the classics. The Northern Isles were about as close as they could've got to the Other, without actually having to leave the shores of Albion. But who was he to scoff? Perhaps, one day, he would come back to live here, by the sea which knew no fixed reference points and which did not judge and compare, but which simply swelled and heaved to the rhythm of the moon, and glistened with pearl dust. He ate the last of his sandwiches. His thermos coffee had long gone cold. The cheese was stale.

He was onto his second candle. He glanced at his watch. Two hours beyond midnight. The darkest point of the night. And not even the ticking of a clock he thought, to remind me that somewhere on this earth, my heart still beats. But it was not really dark.

The east-facing window was a shade of purple. It would be another fine day later. At some point during the night mist had fallen like a curtain across the island. Frame knew that it might not lift for days. And there would be no planes, or even ferries, either in or out, till it did. He sniffed the air and then began to pace the floor-boards. I should've brought a book, he mused, and then he laughed out loud. His laughter sank into the dark shelves of the bookcases, and brought to him a sudden consciousness of being completely alone. He stopped pacing. The wood was silent. It was a sign of incipient lunacy. But there would be no moon tonight. No moon, and no lifting of this oppressive feeling which blanketed the island and filled his chest so that each breath became a mea-sured effort, a breaking down of time inside of himself. He went over to the window and gazed blindly into the white darkness beyond. He tried to imagine where the mist might end, somewhere out over the water, a shifting, ragged sweep of the sea which might lie anywhere between the hard-blown glass of the Rectory window and the coast of Norway. The way of Nor. If I gaze for long enough, he thought, I shall grow irreversibly myopic, until I will be able to look only inside my own head. Every path in this life led to madness.

No-one had stayed in the place since the late 1960s, when some hippies had come up with an agit-prop theatre company and used the Rectory as a radical squat. Reputedly they had cultivated various species of mushroom and herb, both in the rooms and out-side in the garden, and had held strange, naked rituals by the sea's edge. Dancing skin circles around the skeletal rocks. But they had left when winter had come roaring in, and the plants had withered and perished. No-one else had wanted to stay there after that. The place had been left to rack and ruin. Surprisingly, in spite of the prevailing sou-westerlies and the sporadic and perishing north-easterly gales, roof and windows had not fallen in and since no vandals had reached that far north, the Rectory still stood, over a century after its construction, overgrown but essentially intact. I'll not find anything here, he thought. It'll be another of those one-flip sites; one flip of the needle would be all. He would leave whenever he could, cold, hungry and sleep-deprived. He was sleepy right now. Frame's mobile phone lay on the table beside the silver ball of the chronosphere. Now why on earth have I still got that he wondered. It's just a remnant of a past life. I don't need it any more and anyway, the waves don't even reach this far out. He stood up and took the black plastic mobile phone, saw that its battery had run down, slid open the top drawer of the desk and shoved it in. He sat down again.

From beyond the window, from the thin strip of scrubgrass and sand which was all that lay between the Rectory and the sea, Frame felt a swell begin to build. It wasn't something he was able to hear or see. It wasn't really a sensation. All at once, it made him feel smooth and loose, a bit like the way he'd have felt after a work-out or a swim. But beneath it all there was a noise. A scratching sound. At first Frame thought there might be rats in the ceiling and instinctively he ducked, but then he noticed the machines. The chronosphere needle had gone wild and was tearing across the paper in a manner which had never happened before, not even with the subterranean stream. He shivered, and drew his arms around his body. The window was firmly closed, but it was as though it had just swung open. Everything had turned intensely cold. His bones froze. Frame felt fingers slip across his back. The Rector. But something didn't fit. The touch had been that of a woman. Slowly, he turned around.

She was seated in the chair opposite Frame, and was looking at him, and talking in a voice clearer than his own (though just then, he wasn't doing any talking), but somehow, at first, he couldn't make out the meaning of what she was saying. She was speaking in an accent which he recognised as vaguely Orcadian, yet somehow far older. It were as though her breath had been pulled through soil from the deep past, from the long stone slabs which once had danced in circles across the island. He felt no fear. He was no longer cold. Her words emerged into sand.

You look tired, she said.

What's your name? he asked.

She held out her hand and in a movement which seemed quite natural, he rose, bowed and kissed the place just above the line of her knuckles. Her skin was cool, but soft and the taste on his lips was pleasantly salty. Her body was lithe, and beneath her long, grey dress, Frame could see that her breasts were rounded and firm. Her complexion was fair and her lips possessed a faint tinge of violet. She wore a necklace of pearls which, he knew, were real. She had long, soft (he knew it would be soft) hair which fell about her neck in silver tresses. It was not the colour of old age, but of ageless silver. Her eyes held a hint of bemusement – at the sight of him, no doubt – and were a light blue-grey, the colour of the Orcadian sea on a rising, summer tide, early in the morning.

Braga Farquharson is my name.

How long have you been here?

She glanced away, and a distant look came into her eyes, and their movement reminded Frame of the slick of the sea as it moved slowly over pearls and she sighed, so that he could feel the grey dress slip ever so slightly across the cream-coloured skin of her neck.

I was here when Brusa was filled with the creaking bellies of wooden ships.

Longships? he enquired, somewhat astonished.

Herring ships.

Oh.

I was not married to the Rector, but I came to love him. And I was his undoing.

Frame was puzzled. She had almost no eyebrows, and after a while it dawned on him that her body was hairless so that her skin seemed to glow with a dim light.

So... you're not Mrs Farquarson? Yet you took his name. What happened to the Rector? I assume you are referring to the Rector Archibald Farquharson.

Archibald? I was his sister.

Frame rocked back in his chair. Felt the ancient wood curl beneath his spine.

You loved him – as a sister.

As a wife.

He let his breath out, in a stream. The chronosphere needle hit metal.

It was our sin. A very old sin. A Biblical evil. Yet we did not feel evil, Archibald and I. You see, we were of the sea, of the selkie tide, and in the ocean there is no evil and no good. There was never any Eden beneath the waves.

You're a selkie?

She flashed him a look.

Don't insult me, Frame. I am a fin-woman. A mermaid. And where did Farquarson go? He returned to the sea.

And that's where you've come from today?

The shadows grew longer and then shrank, and the cracks in the wall appeared and then vanished in tune with the candle.

She did not answer, but turned her slender neck and he could see that she was gazing towards the window, in the direction of the sea-line. He looked at the empty bookshelves, at the lectern where the one large Bible had sat, the Bible which, he knew, suddenly had turned one stormy, summer night of gospels and knives into the *Book of the Black Art*. The Book which Rector Farquharson had read and imbibed like an oyster, sea-water, and which he had then used to draw the fin-woman away from the hidden place and to imprison her in the library of his wisdom, among the books and the leather and the wood. And in that moment Frame knew that the Rector had performed the ancient ritual of the Fin Folk on a selkie tide, and had become the eternal brother of Braga of the Silver Tresses, and that since the Fin Folk recognise no evil and no good, he had possessed her also as a wife. She had risen from her chair. The table stood between them. Frame was suddenly aware of her gaze directed at him.

You are my seventh.

What?

He had a sense of something sinking in his gut. She had known his name.

She smiled.

Farquharson was my first you understand.

For a moment he thought that he had misheard. Then it occurred to him that he might be losing his mind. Or that he might be asleep. But the fact that the smell of the sea in his nostrils had grown stronger pointed against that.

He heard a strange sound, yet the tune was familiar to his ears. He tried to place it. It was coming from the mobile phone, from inside the drawer. *The Old Man and the Sea.* Yes, that was it. He knew there was no call coming in.

Suddenly she was coquettish. She swirled around as though she were wearing a long ball-gown and not a tight, grey dress.

Do you think I am beautiful? she asked, as she danced on toes light with the notes.

The tune played three times and then stopped, suddenly, in the middle of the fourth cycle. She stopped in mid-flight. The dance was broken. She seemed suddenly distant, and intensely frail. He felt he would be able to snap her in two, like a seahorse, with a simple twist of his arm. He drew breath, and spoke quietly.

You are the most beautiful being I have set eyes upon, in this life or the next.

Her face grew serious.

There is no other life. And I wish to prolong beauty in this one, to extend it so that my eyes shall match the sea forever and so that I shall step outside of time's tyranny. I wish my beauty to be more than merely that which you are able to see.

Where is Farquharson now? he asked, a little tentative after her outburst.

She seemed distracted.

...Farquharson? He is in Hether Blether.

The vanishing courts... he whispered. He was no longer surprised at his knowledge.

She glanced at the window.

It will soon be sunrise. No-one must see me.

No-one can see you, Braga. No-one but me.

She shook her head.

It is the spey-wives I'm afraid of. With their steel bibles, they pierce my eyes like the beaks of the brown bonxie.

A tiny shiver ran through her body, so that her grey dress caught the silver in the dull light of the candle. She went on as though driven by some fast-flowing current.

From before the beginning of time we roamed free through the ocean. Like thoughts we took different forms. Then the metal ships came, and the big nets, and we had to vanish, to go out of time. We no longer sang to men, except in their heads. The Rector set out to debunk everything that had gone before, but gradually, day by day, I sang to him that which he could not hear, and the sea air blew into his lungs and replaced the blood in his veins. He summoned me from the Vanishing Isle, and held me here, in this place.

She swung her arms around her. They were slim, yet he could see that her chest would be ocean strong. Hers was a deceptive frailty.

So many books… and yet, at the end, it was I who took him down.

She looked at Frame with a piteous expression.

I do not want to grow old and ugly like the rest. I will not disappear.

The she became angry.

I will not be an old fin-wife! Never!

Where are the rest of the fin-folk? he asked, quietly.

Vanished, like the Norn, into men's heads, or else turned to fin-wives. They have lost all hope. Or else they are caught in the barbarous, unhearing nets of sea-trawlers, or blackened with oil slicks, or cracked like sea-horses.

She looked him straight in the eye, then glanced away. Had she really read his thoughts? The image of a sea-horse, lying dead and broken on the ocean floor, was powerful and tragic. Or was it he who had read the mind of a mermaid? He ran his fingers through his hair, which once had been long and had been the colour of ripe corn, but which long ago had been cropped short, military-style. Scythed, along with his dreams. Cold sweat beaded his scalp.

I, too have lost hope, many times, he mused, and his voice seemed to come from the end of a long tunnel. There was a pause, and the sound of the waves, massing and then seething back, filled the room. When Braga spoke again, a strange sense of dislocation had settled in the library.

I took one of the hippies awhile back. The rest of them were so far out they didn't even notice.

He found himself basking in her sense of humour. He realised it was the first time in years that he had really enjoyed the company of a woman. Then she opened her mouth, and began to sing.

He found himself behind her eyelids.

Her voice was thin and plaintive, and it rose and fell as she sang the words to a song he didn't immediately recognise, but with whose cadence he felt he was familiar. However, the language seemed very archaic, some old, northern tongue, long-forgotten by all but the dead. He closed his eyes and after a while he was up on a hill-top by an unbroken Odin Stone, the ends of his fingers touching the silhouette bones of one whom he could not see. The wind blew in his hair, and he felt his mouth open and close and no words issued forth.

The song ended. He opened his eyes.

She rose, and Frame rose with her. She moved along the bookcases. Her hand sculpted out the places where books once had sat, and it was as though she were browsing through their vanished pages.

The books are gone, said Frame.

She looked at him, and she was far away, in some distant land beyond the land of the Gor, beyond even the realm of the Finn.

They are invisible, she said.

I will miss you, he said.

He glanced at the chronosphere whose needle had over-reached itself and fractured right down the middle, and at the stereoscope which, he realised, had been emitting a high-pitched, dog frequency howl in the shape of a lenticule, ever since Braga had entered. Then he remembered that in fact she hadn't entered, but had simply appeared, sitting in the chair. He wondered again if perhaps he really was insane. But then, if he was mad then so too were the machines and thence, the whole of science. Several hundred years of lunacy thrown into disarray by a being who had known neither evil nor good and for whom such terms were truly without meaning. For the fin folk the ocean was a dissonant symphony of light. It was beyond logic. Or else, it was the supreme logic. Yet a persistent thought nagged him.

But what of Farquarson? he asked.

She inclined her head, ever so slightly, and though there was no detectable wind in the library, Frame thought he saw the breeze sift through her silvery hair. She smiled, and her smile was of the back rocks, her teeth were the flames of koli lamps. Iron seas, her breath in his mouth. He reeled back feeling suddenly dizzy. The shelves, the room, the Rectory swam around him. The lectern, the steel bible, the pure smell of kirkyard earth.

He was my brother, but he knew it not. We move among human folk, like silver among copper.

The sea was pouring in through the sand of the glass and the walls. Her grey dress was turning to silver, and her cream-white skin, to gold. Around her feet the sea-water was swirling like the caresses of a lover. Then the arms were his arms, and he felt the sea around him, inside him. His hair was long and silver, and swept around his shoulders as it had thirty years earlier when he had cultivated and partaken of the agit-prop mushrooms and gone on the trip from whence he had never returned. As it had, a hundred years before that, when he had come to this place as Rector, as scientific Dundonian Christian intent on reform and improvement, and as it had, a thousand years before that, when he had returned with the bone ships from a Holy Land steeped in the blood of fresh crucifixions.

You are my seventh, she whispered, and her whisper was the warm, prevailing sou-westerly.

The candle blew out.

I am your seventh, Braga whispered, and her whisper was the icy, winter nor-easterly.

We grow young through our mortal lives, each one longer than the span of the ancient books. We are become redemption itself. Together, fin and human, we have ridden the njuggle across the span of the oceans and we have vanquished the tyranny of Michael and of Eden. Through our love of unspoken words, the ocean has swept away the King of the Cross and now we may farm freely beneath the sea.

She was facing him, he could feel her cold fish breath, and yet he no longer felt it so, and their lips joined and her long, finned body pressed against his. Her lips tasted of reef coral. Her heart beat a tide against his chest, and he was drowned in her blood. Inside him, her bones danced green withershins in the shape of an earth-curse. Her thoughts came in whispers that were like kisses. The great underground chambers of the Fin King's palace flashed before his eyes, the pillars, the arched roof-beams, the swaying, dancing ganfer forms and in the deepest chamber of all, he saw a room which was exactly like the Rectory library. And in that watery room, so like the inside of an enormous shell, he saw Braga and the dark stranger who once had been a Norse warrior, embrace and lie down together, naked in the clear liquid. Every seventy years, the span of a human life, every seven warts of the oar, she returned and reclaimed him, his body, his soul, and so had they avoided both the fate of the Fin-folk, which was to grow immeasurably aged, and the destiny of humankind, which was to turn to kirkyard earth.

My love, do you not remember sailing along the Eastern shore in the long, long ships of King Karl? Do you remember the look in the eyes of Earl Paul the Blind? The burning stink of Thorkel Flayer as his skin leapt from his body into the flames? Can you not feel the wind as it blows across our bodies as we lie between the tidemarks, on the skerry rocks of Eynhallow? We have loved through many ages of men, and yet, in our hearts, we grow young. For the sea washes away all sins and only knowledge remains. And it is the knowledge of the waves, of the white spume. Ours is a pure history.

And all at once he was standing by a wheelie-stane, on his lips the rub of an old, clay pipe, its stem worn to the weave of his lips. And from the endless sky which swung like a cold, white flame across the islands, he heard the dead-shak song of a quail, and he knew that if the fin-woman did not come soon, he too would lie with a Bible 'neath his chin. Aye, he had known Braga Farquharson when he had been Rector of this place, but he had known her long before, in the darkness of fishermen's cottages where the lik-strae dust bore the sole prints of a mortal father and where their mother, hidden till the time of the spa ben lest the peerie folk should cast their spells, sought out in her dreams the feather of a black cock to crow awa the trows.

He knew that outside the sky would be lightening and the waves tripping, one over the next like the waves of men who had come and gone by the water's edge, and that up on the hill the light would stretch and pull along the tall stones which were incised with the initials of long-dead interlopers. There was blood in the ocean; the ocean was blood. He tasted it in his mouth, felt it run along the lines of his back. His legs which once had been stone but which now were turning like the world and would take him ever northwards, seven times and more, out past Fetlar and Baliasta to the crags of Gisk and Sekk and then further, up to the White Sea where those who had known neither Eden nor Fall dwelt in peace still. He was sinking in the white metal seas, he was skinned again in the silver and gold of the skies. And in that liquid moment, which stretched beyond the ends of time and space, he felt the machines which he had abandoned, become molten and explode slowly into air, and he knew that he would spend eternity in the cold ocean which he had never really left.

He stumbled and reached out to stop himself, but then he realised that he had already fallen and that he was swimming away, out through the cracks in the walls which had opened up like sea rivers, and away from Brusa Island, from the here-and-now that has never been real, and into the ocean from which everything comes and to which, at length, all things must return. And that the ancient fin-man who, in this world, had been known as Frame and his sister-wife who many centuries earlier had taken the name Braga, once again and forever would be as one.

Epilogue

One week later, after the fog had lifted, a pilot flying a Britten Norman Islander over Brusa Island noticed that Frame's car had not moved from near the Rectory, and informed the police. It was rumoured (though never confirmed in official reports) that when the local policeman had opened the Rectory door it had taken more than the usual amount of effort, and that when, finally, it did open, sea-water had gushed through the doorway almost sweeping the policeman off his feet. A freak flood on a selkie tide had engulfed part of Brusa Island that night. No body was ever found. The Rectory was declared dangerous, and an order was issued from Kirkwall for its demolition. Somehow, the order has not yet been carried out. Something about the machines needing repair, or the demolition teams being ill with backache. The dead spey-wives know better.

Glossary

bonxie	Great Skua – dark brown bird that has been known to attack people
Britten Norman Islander	9-seater propellor plane that flies from island to island throughout the Northern Archipelagos
daberlacks	seaweed
dead-shak	the song of the common quail, said to presage death
ganfer	ghost that appears when a person is about to die
koli lamp	a small open iron lamp which burned fish oil
lik-strae	the straw of the death-bed which was burned after the body had been removed from it

njuggle	Shetlandic mythical water-horse
spa ben	prophecy bone; the condyle between the thigh-bone and shank of a sheep. In Shetland, it was used to predict the sex of an unborn child
trows	trolls (often interchangeable with fairies)
warts	strokes (of the oar). It is said that a fin-man can sail from Orkney to the coast of Norway with seven strokes of the oar
wheelie-stanes	traditional resting-places for coffin-bearers on the way to the graveyard
withershins	widdershins

My thanks to Alistair Peebles, George Gunn and Leslie Manson and to the Orkney *Skald* which breathes within us all. Also, to *The Mermaid Bride and other Orkney Folk Tales*, by Tom Muir, *The Folklore of Orkney and Shetland*, by Ernest Marwick and to the hidden, unending tale of the *Orkneyinga*, by the dark stranger.

SHARK ATTACK

Curt Rosenthal

SHARK ATTACK

Curt Rosenthal

AT SIXTY-YEARS OLD Tino is fit and strong with a thick head of slicked grey hair. From the neck of his starched T-shirt, a heavy cloth napkin drapes over his sturdy chest. A wizened dyed-in-the-wool Italian gamer, he speaks down at his plate twisting a fork of fettuccini.

'The bitch hit it rich on number seven Tommy.'

Mom's love-groove skipped tracks like a scratched record, bringing Tino into my life when I was eleven. Six years later mom left him, so I left her. Took a Greyhound to New York City the day I turned seventeen.

Tino shakes his head at his half-eaten plate, belabouring a subject I can't understand why he'd think I'd want to hear about. 'Lucky number seven all right,' he chuckles sadly, putting his hand on my arm. His ruby pinky ring reflects the flickering candlelight. In a fist his other hand covers his mouth while he chews, 'I wonder how many times that whore had to roll the craps dice to find her this new piece of dog meat...'

Growing up those years in Ohio with Tino were the best times I had so far in this life. He's the closest person I have to a father, hell, to a friend.

* * *

I'm on my stomach drifting in and out of consciousness as the morning sun rises over Orient Bay. A breeze scratches my sunburn and I open my eyes. The shrub-grass at the rear of the desolate beach arches in a restful curve toward the ocean. I'm still drunk from our late night at the casino, so when I turn my head to find Tino I do so carefully. Shading the brightness with my forearm I see the outline of a waiter balancing a tray. Tino greets me with a frozen Pina Colada, frosting my hand like a slap in the face. He raises his religiously.

'To another day of relaxation.'

I'm most concerned about Tino's condition this morning after watching him black out last night and then dragging him out here to sleep. He thinks nothing of picking up drinking at nine in the morning. And there's no sign of fatigue. No visible decay in the crazy bull. I guess I can't help but love the man. For the past ten years the third week in March shines on my calendar like the lazy Caribbean sun.

I barely speak, but words roll out, 'Thank you for another great visit. Even though one of these times you're gonna kill me with all this.'

Tino's up on his feet giving his face to the sun, eyes closed, welcoming the morning with outstretched arms holding his mixed-drink like some libertine Christ figure. With a careful expressionless face he replies, 'Any time son.' He adjusts his trunks up on his rigid bloated belly. Pulling them high enough that he's nearly tucked in his gold medallion. 'We gotta live before we die my boy. Ain't that right?' He starts to twist side-to-side, warming up, like I saw him do on the first tee when we went golfing years ago. I tell him earnestly, 'I'm glad to see you're enjoying yourself with me.'

Tino pats my head like when I was eleven as he sits back down facing me, 'And the trip's not done yet you know. We still got one more night together. Who knows what fun we're gonna have.'

We knock plastic cups and recline in our cushioned chairs. I cool back slushy pineapple mix and rum to a newborn steel drum rhythm in the distance. Tino turns to me, 'You know Tommy... I'm getting rid of the timeshare while we're down here this year.' I look at Tino to make sure he's kidding. He turns his head and stares at the ocean, 'I didn't know how to tell you.'

I have no reply.

Tino turns to me, but now I look away, out to the clear-blue water I know I might not see again for a long time.

'I understand our trips here mean a lot to you,' he continues, 'You know they do to me too. It's our meeting place. I watched you grow up down here. I'm glad I could give this to you all these years. But it's the right time to leave it behind. What we have together here, the memories will never leave us.'

Right away I know we'll never see each other again, but I need to ask, 'Will you find another place?'

'Don't look so beat-up Tommy. I'm gonna get a pile of cash off the sale and clean up my mortgage. Let's end it with a bang and move on. Time to move on.'

I think about my youth. St Maarten was a location on the map Tino and I felt worldly travelling to, a hideaway from our lives. I always thought it was a perfect place for us, its unique inter-changeable name depending if you were on the Dutch or French side – Sint Maarten or Saint Martin – represented our separate worlds that converged when we met down here.

By the look I give Tino I hope he doesn't think I'm all broken up inside. He shouldn't know how I feel. This must be as hard for him as it is for me, so I urge him with my most sincere confidence, 'I think you're making a good decision. Time to move on.'

Since we all split up and I made it to New York I rarely leave the place. Haven't been back to Ohio. Tino is forty years at his reliable union job with the Teamsters. He'd never step foot in a big city. We only talk on the phone once a month or so. Tino says it's a hobby for teenage girls.

I suck the pulp from the bottom of my plastic cup and turn to Tino, 'Hey, why don't we go in the water.' He waves me off, 'You go ahead. That fettuccini's runnin' through me.'

By the time I near the ocean I'm at a run. I dive through a crashing wave. When I surface I swim fifteen hard strokes out. I'd swim to the middle if I could, and keep swimming, but I'm winded, so I let myself float. I lean my head back submerging my ears. Everything is silent. I'm alone. If I drowned no one would know. Maybe Tino. Looking to the sky I close my eyes. I could float like this forever... but I've got to take a piss.

I tread with only my legs so I can drop my shorts – I let it stream.

Fully relieved, trunks below my knees, a heavy set of waves roll in. Treading and wiggling to tuck myself in I manoeuvre against them. A gush crosses my legs. A living-moving-circling presence... Shark!

My legs are shackled. Do I pull up my suit and die, or tear it off and swim for my life? I thrash, splash in a shocked panic, twist my body, yank my shorts down and flutter them into the undertow.

'Hey! Cool it fella. We won't bite.'

My tsunami settles. I'm breathing hard, floating naked between two bobbing snorkelers. My chest heaves, gasping for air. 'Holy shit. I thought you guys were a shark.' Taking her mask off, a silky blonde giggles at me, 'I thought you were some kind of drowning epileptic.'

'I was watching you pee,' the other garbles through her mouthpiece, removing it and her mask together. Cocoa-smooth skin glistening in the sun, she pinches water from her almond-shaped browns, her hand shimmies loose delicate cropped matted hair. She looks to her partner sarcastically, then back at me, 'You musta drained a litre fella.'

The two chuckle softly. They share the accent of my favourite coffee bar waitress near my apartment. I try to respond, 'I... I... Yeah, I had to go pretty bad.'

So I went. Now I'm their damn marine show. A fucking Leviathan.

The dark-haired one continues, 'Where'd your costume go?'

'My costume?'

The blonde holds her mask to her face. She dips in the water then flips back up. 'Shark musta torn 'em off.'

I wish I could laugh but I'm still reeling from the image of Tino dragging my nude dismembered body over the sand.

The blonde asks, 'You American?'

'I am. And you two are from Australia.'

'Sharp for a Yank,' she winks at me.

These two are the best looking girls I've ever seen in my life. Both are tan. Tan like they live in the sun.

'Tommy!' Tino stands at the water's edge holding his stomach like he's about to give birth, 'Tommy! We got to get back to the unit pronto!'

I yell back, 'I'm busy!'

I can't believe this is happening. He doesn't relent, 'One-hundred apologies. A million. But let's go now!'

Tino turns and heads to the chairs.

The three of us float in silence.

'Hurry up Tommy,' the blonde says smugly.

'Yeah, looks like your old man's got to lay a steamer,' the other adds, no sooner submerging for an encore.

I don't give her a chance because I hit a hard crawl to the shore. As I cross the sand and approach Tino I can only imagine the morning rays off the ocean glistening my pimpled slacker's ass. Whether amused or haunted, I'll never know the girl's reaction, but it can't compare to Tino's as he looks up from zipping his beach bag.

Like I'm a boxer returning to my corner between rounds – bloodied, humiliated – Tino gathers me in to him and sits me down. He throws a towel over my shoulders. I'm getting my ass kicked out there, but his strong hands are encouraging and hold up my defeated head to his face, his grin is greedy.

'You're my hero.'

'What are you talking about?'

'A god damn fucking Adonis.'

'What's going on?'

'What's going on is you was having sex with those gorgeous girls I was eyeing near the snorkeling shack. Holy Cannoli! Doin' them must have been like heaven.'

'No. You got it wrong.'

'There's nothing wrong about that son.'

Tino puts his arm around me like he's my new best friend. In all these years I've never felt him this close. He looks me in the eyes, and in his proudest most serious fatherly tone tells me, 'You been a shy kid ever since I known you, but this is nothing to be ashamed of. This here is our happiest moment Tommy. Even if we're not genuine father and son, I'm proud to be the guy to tell you this... today you are finally a man.'

*　*　*

'Luck be a lady tonight.' Tino tosses two twenty-five-dollar chips on the felt and winks at the dealer across the table. He pats my cheek, 'I ever tell ya you're a good looking kid Casanova?'

The stagnant plume from Tino's cigarette envelopes my head and burns my eyes. I nip an under-boozed Rum and Coke, not enjoying it, but Tino shouldn't have to drink alone. As the dealer lays out the hand Tino tells him, 'You should have seen this kid make me proud this morning. I never knew it but my son here takes after his pops. A living Don Juan.'

I should really come clean on the events of this morning, but I can't do that to Tino, it's not worth it. Let the guy be proud. Maybe through my conquest he's living it up for himself a bit. This part of my life is over in a day anyhow. If it makes him happy, when we're gone he'll remember me as a man. His hero.

I pat Tino on the back, suddenly sad distance has grown between us already. I tell him, 'Win some tonight... You know, I'm not feeling so great. I think I'm gonna head up to the room.'

As I step away Tino grabs my arm, places a Merit between his lips and scrapes up a flame. As he lights his smoke he casually slants his head across the room. He shifts his glance to check if I see what he sees.

The blonde is significantly taller than I would have guessed. A princess from Outback-stock. Someday she'll breed Olympic athletes. Well proportioned, perfectly symmetrical, all the necessary angles, round everywhere else. She shimmies into the room knowing everyone is watching.

In her shadow flirting with the Pit Boss the buttery dark one radiates naughty-bird sex appeal. A cut-off jean skirt barely covers her cheeks. She looks drunk. Sassy. On the make and a touch out-of-control. Her jet-black hair is messy like she was recently pleasured. And I can't keep my eyes off the roundest-firmest-perkiest most delicious breasts she's taken obvious measures not to restrain by a bra.

'You had yourself two gifts from the heavens this morning,' Tino whispers to me, then tries to get their attention with a fanatical wave.

'Stop doing that!' I pull down at his arm. 'I'm gonna get them over here,' he explains, annoyed I'd question his tactics.

'Why would you want to do that?' I ask.

''Cause you're gonna convince one of them your old man needs taking care of on his last night down here. How about the blonde Tommy... How was she? Although the little dark one looks more likely to play around.'

'Please stop. Sorry to ruin your night, but I have to go to bed.' Tino shakes his head without breaking his stare, 'Go to bed? C'mon, not now Tommy. What you did men like me go to their graves dreaming about.'

I make my move to the exit and Tino grabs my arm expecting he's finally called my bluff, like I was goofing on him and I'd love nothing more than to watch him gamble in his smoke and get him laid. He gets up from his chair to straighten his belt, expecting an introduction.

I take another step toward the back door. 'Tommy, don't love 'em and leave 'em. If anyone, you should know how it feels.' Tino looks at me with pleading eyes and settles-up in front of me blocking my path.

'Let the old guy have a shot.'

'I don't get what makes you think you have a shot?'

'You was a virgin before this trip. Am I right?'

'How would you know?'

'I wasn't born yesterday. Truthfully I was wiping my brow you wasn't one of them queers.'

'You never answered me. With all respect Tino, what makes you think you can so easily do to them what I did with them?'

'This is exactly why you was a virgin so long. You gotta know girls like those. With all respect, I lived with one for six years.'

I blew my chance to leave; they're walking toward us. I'm right where I don't want to be, feeling queasy in a pile of smoke between Tino, them and my lie. From the side of my mouth I tell him, 'Pretend we don't see them. I'll make sure the night ends up the way you want it to.'

Chin in his chest Tino says, 'Sounds a little loose to me.'

I almost yell, 'Please!'

'I gotta trust you know what you're doing...' He consents.

'Look like we're playing cards,' I tell him and lean on the table expecting to stave Tino off briefly enough to jet-out as soon as the girls pass. I ask him, 'So would the Caribbean be an easier place to count cards than at big money tables at places like Caesars in Vegas?'

He turns at me like I'm stupid, 'Tommy, you know I'd never play Caesars.'

I quip back sharply, 'Wherever you play!'

I shift on my feet nervous as hell. Fists clenched, I close my eyes and vow if they get near me I'll punch those two square in the face rather than suffer humiliation. I smell shampoo mixed with a French perfume popular here on the island. I'm too weak in the knees for violence. My sweaty palms loosen. My pits itch.

They're breathing on me.

'Jo, I'm thinking you should stop and play here.' Her voice makes the hairs on my neck stand. Jo is the blonde. She quips back to the dark velvet vamp, 'All right then, I'll take the house in a hand.' Jo settles into a chair at the other side of the table. The other stands over her like I do Tino. They're an arms-length away, luckily blocked by other gamblers and a pack of men who meandered over for a few free stares.

They haven't noticed me. And if I move now I'll draw attention to myself. I should be optimistic they have no idea who I am. I was wet then and they're drunk now.

Jo pushes out all her chips at once. Quick math tells me no less than two thousand dollars. She orders a whisky from the waitress. The breasty-one heaves out her full chest holding a beer she carried in with her. I can't help but join the chorus of stares, although if she catches me I'm dead in the water. I sidestep behind Tino's head just in case. Measuring his stack of chips Tino peers at how many dollars Jo wagers and recklessly pushes out the same amount.

Tino turns to me with the most shit eating grin I've seen since his prized photograph with Dolly Parton in front of the kaleido-scope fountain at the grand opening of the Bellagio. With big time money at play, pursed lips and subtle clearance nods acknowledging it's time for me to break the ice, Tino is as game as he gets.

I whisper, 'No chance old man.'

Cards slide out the shoot before he can answer and make their way left to right. Tino is smoking faster than I've ever seen and starts tapping his fingers on the table like a savant. He's trying to impress, but visibly nervous as hell. The highest I've seen him wager was seventy-five dollars.

Tino and Jo are dealt a King and Queen respectively. Tino looks across the table to Jo and says, 'We'll take Kings and Queens all night. Ain't that right?'

She takes a sip of her whisky, 'We will mista. Surely will.'

Tino continues. 'What's your name sweetheart?' I cringe.

She smiles. 'Joanna.'

'And your friend?'

'This is Maxa.'

'Cute. Cute girls. I'm Tino Zanetti. This here is Tommy.'

'Pleasure boys.' Joanna politely reaches across the table and shakes Tino's hand, then offers her hand to me. I shake it. She doesn't recognize me. Tino is a dead man. But maybe I'm in the clear.

Maxa grins at me, then Tino, and kicks back her beer. She steps behind the table with her hand outstretched to reach me. I look at her hand for what feels like minutes before dreadfully lifting my gaze to hers. She grins, pulls me toward her and wets my ear with a soft whisper, 'See any sharks in here?'

Feeling weak I balance myself on the table. The waitress passes. Maxa orders a Vodka and Tonic with a twist of lime. I neatly shuffle to my spot behind Tino. He winks at me satisfied with our situation, unaware I hate him and am miserable for getting into this situation on our last night together.

Between the big money on the table, his excellent first card, hers, them bonding over it, and the intimate contact with a gorgeous twenty-something-year-old girl, Tino's too aggressive for the subdued Caribbean tables when he starts to bellow, 'How 'bout a couple Aces swimming down the pipe for sweet Jo and old Tino!'

'Hit us baby,' the girls mock in a tone reminiscent of this morning.

Tino drops his open-hand on the felt like a gavel – Joanna is sharply delivered an Ace of Diamonds. He pounds his hand one more time when his card is laid down – Ace of Clubs. Tino roars, 'Double Blackjack! Gotta tell 'em what you want girls. Tell 'em or they won't give it to ya.'

'That's right! Tell 'em Tino baby!' Joanna shouts. The girls cheer and high five Tino. He pulls in his winnings and stands. 'We ain't going to bed tonight girls.'

* * *

After seven rounds of shots they haven't mentioned what happened, but I continue to balance on the edge of humiliation with every word. The girls feed us more shots. I'm about to be sick. Maxa holds a beer in front of me, 'Wash 'em down to keep 'em down is how we do it Down Under...'

Nearly two thousand dollars of Tino's chips are scattered like puzzle pieces on the bar. Maxa literally pours beer down my throat. Tino occupies Joanna's numb expression with detailed stories about his seeping old tattoos, which at this point are more like a Rorschach test. To complete the gallery tour Tino unbuttons his shirt.

Maxa points at his left pectoral, 'What's that one?'

Tino looks at them proud. 'A shark. Picked it up in sixty-three. My Marine battalion was The Killer Sharks. We were mean sons-of-bitches.'

'Tommy saw a shark this morning,' Maxa says. 'I'm sure he told you about it.'

I nod at him as if to tell him I sure did and he should move to a new topic. He begins to laugh and asks me, 'A shark in Carribean waters?'

They're all laughing. Looking at me. Expecting me to answer. Maxa burns her eyes into mine breathing fire from her devil lips. Tino's face is distorted – a fleshy beast. His arm curls around Joanna to keep him from falling. She laughs without noise – lifeless, pale, intoxicated.

* * *

I come to in a haze. White tile surrounds me. I'm in my underwear. My soiled clothes are bunched in the corner. Tino holds my head from splashing into the drowning toilet. I puke. The room spins, my eyes cry. The hard floor hurts my knees. Chunks fill my mouth and pour out. My stomach is acid, shredded bile.

I ask, 'Are they gone?'

'They're in the other room,' he tells me impatiently.

'What time is it? How did I get in our bathroom?'

'Take a shower. Or go into your room and crawl in bed.'

I plead, 'We have to get away from them.'

Annoyed with me Tino says, 'Don't be dumb.'

'I mean it. They're not what you think they are...' I fall back against the wall drooling, staring at Tino. My ribs feel broken. Life sucked from me – hollow, raw. Barely speaking I try to reason with him, 'Just tell them to leave. Do it for me.'

Tino gets down on a knee at my level and says, 'Tommy, they're two silly drunk girls with cute little accents who like to have a good time. I know better than anyone how to handle this situation. I'm grateful you paved the path. Always remember that. I'm proud of you.'

Tino stands. He is without his shirt eager to get back to the girls, but cleaning my mess in uncertain motions not wanting to appear insensitive.

He stands over me to leave and says, 'You'll sober up at the beach tomorrow before we get on the plane. It's our last day. We'll spend it sharing stories thanking the Big Man our last trip here ended with us getting laid. And then I got fifteen hundred dollars to spend on you. This is the best going away present we could ever ask for.'

'What did they tell you about this morning?'

Without answering he leaves me on the floor and closes the door. My eyes shut.

I'm in the water on my back looking at the sky and can only hear quiet. I'm alone. If I drowned no one would know.

Not even Tino.

I hear a voice, Tino's voice. We are on his porch. He looks

younger, very alive. I'm writing a story for school. He just got home from work. He speaks to me, 'I'm going away tomorrow. I hope I will see you again Tommy, but I'm not sure if your mom will allow it. Maybe we'll catch up with each other again some-time if we can work it out. Maybe your mom will let us visit down in St. Maarten, just the two of us. Don't want to miss the fun we have down there.'

My mother walks up the drive and he stops talking. She leads him in the house.

* * *

Bright light sprays through the window and covers my back. Morning is cruel to hangovers greeted faced-down on tile. My body is sweaty, the inside dry. Climbing to my feet pain stabs my stomach. Aching legs and a pounding head bumps me through the tight hall-way to the living room. It's empty. The television is on but there is no trace of life. The open balcony doors let in a fresh breeze.

I find a bottle of water in the refrigerator and pour it on my head, my face, down my throat. Ready for whatever the day brings I look across the balcony, the rising sun over the ocean reminds me it's our last day. Time to find Tino and go to the beach. Live the final hours to their fullest, then leave it all behind.

I walk out on the balcony to breathe the air. It's clean and clear and fills me with strength. In the corner Tino lies naked on a lounge chair. The sun shines on him, bright – he's glowing.

Tino is dead.

There's no doubt about it. His wallet is open on the table, money gone. A smile covers his face bigger than I ever thought a man was capable of smiling, all the way around his head if that's possible. He was taken for more than his winnings by those sharks I saw in the water yesterday morning – credit cards, jewellery – but it looks like he got what he wanted in return.

THEY GROW THE ICE THICK

Marcie Hume

THEY GROW THE ICE THICK

Marcie Hume

MAGNUS MARKÚSSON STANDS seven feet, three inches tall; he is taller than two horses, the people in Iceland often say. At the age of 33, Magnus has never had a girlfriend, but he knows that his woman exists somewhere in the world. Magnus would prefer a lady who is brawny in build and light in character; someone who can bear seven or so of his oversized babies.

On the eve of The World's Strongest Man Competition, Magnus sits in a diner with two plates of pancakes and maple syrup. He waits for a journalist for the Stout Mountain Press, with whom his publicist has arranged an interview at the Renaissance Diner in Midtown Manhattan. He feels bigger and more triumphant than ever in Manhattan, but remains at ease; from what he can tell, New York City is a bit like Reykjavík. Both cities are somewhat grey and packed with mostly short people, but Manhattan is powerful and mysterious, and, from what he could tell on his walk from the hotel four blocks away, at least twice as large. Also, the buildings seem to be quite a bit higher.

The diner is crowded, with benches dressed tightly in faux red leather. An entire wall is made of windows, and Magnus looks alternately out the glass and at the perfect bite-size triangles of pancake that he has successfully created. The diner is more than half full, with several tables of women Magnus's age sipping coffees and tittering like jackhammers. There are businessmen, kids, and old people. Every place in the world is basically the same, Magnus thinks. Looking around at the men in suits, the women in tight shirts, he feels surrounded by a fast reality and finds the diner beautiful and exciting. He slides his hand through his coarse blond hair and flexes his feet back under the table.

For Magnus, there could be nothing more magnificent than the thought of a classy New York City journalist who will write an eloquent article about him. At first, he imagined her as a slender bombshell whose cropped shirt would reveal a tanned midsection, but then he rationalized: she won't look like the women on television. She is no MTV journalist. He must remember that sometimes the most brilliant, truly stimulating women are not models; this is common information. Whatever form she takes, in essence she will undoubtedly be luminous and mesmerizing. Magnus's eyes close for a moment as the syrup seeps between his broadened, stumpy teeth.

When Sandra comes rushing in the front entrance her large purse wedges between herself and the metal frame, keeping her stuck there for several seconds. Once she finally breaks free, she instinctively looks down at the sides of her purse, murmuring to God that the fine imitation leather is unharmed. Sandra is simultaneously solid and soft, and carries the female equivalent of a spare tyre. She smells vaguely of paper. Magnus looks up as she slides a pale hand, engorged with water-retention, over the side of her bag. To Magnus, Sandra is an exact duplicate of several other women in the diner, but from the first instant he finds her enticing and moderately burly. Magnus figures she has the right build to cancel out some of his largeness genes, and black, tightly curled hair which mixed with his own genes would give their children dishwater-brown hair.

When Sandra looks up from her purse, she notices first the jaw of Magnus, then the shoulders, then the light blue eyes which croon at her in a different language. She is not sure what Icelandic sounds like, but she is sure, looking now at Magnus's pale lips, that it sounds sugary and satisfying. His shirt is perhaps an eighties squash jersey, thick white fabric with blue and purple triangles covering the sleeves. But she reminds herself that he is from another time and another place... well no, really just another place, and she will have to give him some leeway with fashion and other cultural matters.

Since she was given this assignment last week, she has been imagining him daily. As she walks towards his booth, she thinks momentarily of the photo in her bathroom: the slightly-squatting Magnus, whose image she has examined for seven straight nights while brushing her teeth. This is the brute whose manly wiles have yet to be tamed by any woman... or anyway, she imagines they haven't, probably. But Sandra, in her deepest, most frantic desire, knows that she could domesticate this beast. With Magnus's strange exquisiteness and crowded torso by her side, Sandra would never have to answer to the meddling inquires of old prep school acquaintances whom she encounters regularly on the Upper East Side. With Magnus as her plus one, she could attend social and business functions with a renewed and unfaltering confidence. Magnus could change her; he could be the huge block on which she stands to elevate herself to new heights.

'Are you Mr Markússon?' she says, clutching her purse to her bosom with both hands. She smells something extremely peculiar, but does not want to look distracted by trying to place it and instead stares into Magnus's eyes twice as forcefully.

'Yays.'

'Hello, Sandra Blaustone! Hi, it's nice to see you, how are you?'

'Yays – I ordered.' Magnus holds up his fork with a floppy triangle of sugar-soaked pancake. For a moment, he looks like a muscular two-year-old.

'Oh, yeah? Alright, well that's fine, I'll have a look, I can be quick.' Sandra is shaking slightly, but she masks it easily with languid movements of her plush limbs. Magnus stares at the thick curls of dark hair that end just at the folds of skin on her neck. He wonders if a city girl could ever even consider someone like himself. But in the realm of self-confidence, he uses the same techniques as when he is lifting cars on his shoulders: you are big, you are strong, you are the best. He thinks this over and over to himself as Sandra glances over the menu, and he finally says:

'I ordered you a fish.'

Sandra doesn't know if Magnus is joking, and so she executes her seamless situational protocol: she stares downwards at the menu and waits. Magnus says nothing, looking straight at her, and so she carefully and solemnly mutters: 'Oh... oh.'

When she looks up, Magnus is staring at her breasts. Sandra likes the way his face stays completely still, expressionless. Or maybe she doesn't *like* it, but it's interesting, if not somewhat tawdry. But on second thought, oh yes, she likes it.

'Do you eat fish?' he asks.

'I do, I do, sure. Women have trouble eating enough protein. I mean, not trouble eating it, but they generally don't eat enough of it. I mean, that's what they say, now anyway, but they used to tell us to pack in a lot of carbs, and now, you know... so...'

'Have you ever tried dried fish?' Magnus asks. Sandra thinks she can sense excitement in his voice as he struggles to discharge the words *dried fish*.

'Um... I don't know that we've got that... I don't think we do... well, I'm sure in some specialty shop or something.' Her mouth forms a smile uneasily. To Magnus it appears honest and poised.

He pulls a clear plastic package out of his trousers. The smell arrives immediately at Sandra's face; her eyes fill up with tears and the muscles in her nose contract, contorting her face into a recoiled flinch. She wonders if the smell comes out in the laundry.

'It is translated really as *hard fish*, but I say dried fish, that's also what it is. It's good for you,' Magnus says, smiling for the first time. His teeth are perfectly even and flat, like a combine, she thinks, not sure what a combine does, but fairly confident that they must use them on the vast and chilly terrain of Iceland. She has a fleeting vision of Magnus running through a field of brown winter grass, his thighs stiff and pale, his body charged with a life-time of fish consumption. This dried fish smell might be something she could get used to. She tells herself to remember to say *hard fish*, as this will be more correct, and hopefully impressive. She looks up to Magnus's eyes, trying to unwrinkle her face.

Magnus tears off a piece of the fish and hands it to Sandra, who chews it brightly, eyebrows raised.

'Wow! It's like... gum... it's so chewy...'

'This is what keeps me so strong. This is why Icelanders are so smart and beautiful,' he says with a little laugh, although Sandra senses that apart from the outward giggle, he is disastrously serious. 'Did you know how beautiful Icelandic women are? I'm sure some-one has told you. They are the most beautiful women in the world. I got to lift six of them on a board once for a Strongman competition in Keflavík... which is near Reykjavík... it's where the airport is.'

Sandra tears off a corner of her napkin and folds her arms over her abdomen.

'Your English is very good.' Her stomach turns inside. She once again notices Magnus staring at her breasts.

'But they all look the same, you know. And who needs it.' That's right, who needs it, she tells herself with a jolt of self-buoyancy. Sandra leans, nearly sultry, onto one hand, leaving the other draped across herself. 'I'm sorry that I'm staring at your bouncies,' Magnus continues. 'I know I'm staring. Forgive me. They're so nice.'

Sandra feels delirious and reckless. Does the declaration of guilt absolve Magnus' gawking? Is that the rule? Though if she pardons him for staring just because of his frankness, maybe that is part of his master plan; but can she assume deviousness from such an innocuous animal? Magnus stares on. Sandra has an impulse to grab his enormous head in her hands, but she gathers herself instantaneously and moves forward.

'It's alright, Mr Markússon. I'll just start with some questions, if that's alright.'

'Yays.' Magnus wraps up the dried fish and puts it in his pocket as Sandra pulls out a small spiral notebook from her purse.

'So you have not been to the United States before, is that right?' she asks.

'Yays – I mean no, I have not been – I have never been before. I am nervous. And I get nervous talking to reporters.'

'Journalist,' Sandra says softly, but her modification goes unnoticed. She looks at the plates of pancakes. Magnus loads two triangles onto his fork and inserts them into his mouth like a machine.

As Magnus begins to talk on unleashed about articles that have been written about him, pancake drops twice in one sentence from his teeth. Just as he gets to the end of his fourth sentence, a small Italian man arrives with an oval platter of French fries, lettuce leaves and a whole salmon, about the size of the platter, still with its skin and head.

Sandra looks down at the plate and grabs the bottle of ketchup, submerging the head of the bottle in the flesh of her hand.

'You get nervous with journalists? Even though you've been doing interviews for a long time?'

'Yays, I started out very young – when I was six a reporter for *Morgunbladeið* came to the farm when we had a horse with five legs.'

Sandra's hand grows red from the attempted unscrewing of the ketchup bottle. But she does not allow the exertion to show on her face. She must keep a steady stream of controlled confidence aimed at Magnus's forehead: this, she knows, will pull him towards her. She smiles at Magnus, her lips rising high enough to show the shade of yellow just under her gums.

'Put your weight into it,' Magnus says.

'What?'

'Lean into it – think with your back.'

'Okay,' Sandra says, moving forward quickly, pretending the bottle isn't there. 'That's a nice word, Morgunbla... something... sorry... is that a newspaper?'

'It just means morning paper. They did a half-page story about the horse. But I do have a website, also.'

'Wow!' Sandra expresses revelation at this humdrum piece of information, thinking that a stab at a little flattery can't do any harm. She tilts her head up to make her chin less heavy and notice-able. He might be staring into her eyes now, although logically, she knows it is doubtful.

'My cousin created it. It has a counter at the bottom, to see how many people have, what, hit it, is that right?'

'... Yes.'

'Do you want me to try that for you?' As Magnus points at the ketchup bottle, his hand remains poised and strapping, one finger several inches away from the cap.

'Yes, thank you. But just remember, I loosened it for you!' Sandra quips, letting out a loud chuckle before immediately becoming embarrassed. Sandra watches as Magnus grips the cap. His hand doesn't envelope the bottle: it dominates it. Sandra's mouth opens slightly.

'Yays, and it was last at something like 50,000 people who have seen the site. So that is about 18% of the population of Iceland.'

'That's a lot of people.'

'It is. It is.'

'But that could be people from anywhere in the world. It wouldn't have to be people in Iceland.'

'Hm. Okay well yays, you're right, I'd never thought of it. Okay.'

Magnus is embarrassed; he must seem so small to her. Sandra thinks she can hear the glass bottle bending and creaking under the force of Magnus's muscle, and the skin on his face matches the shade of the bottle, which has not yet been opened. Magnus hides the bottle underneath the edge of the table.

Sandra's lip begins to quiver, but she does not know why. Magnus glances at her chin as it lightly vibrates, and for the first time notices the clumps of hair sprouting from Sandra's chin. He is suddenly afraid; he does not know what it means. He puts the bottle between his knees and makes a small prayer to God that it will open.

'Are the people in Iceland proud? I mean, let's say the women, those women you were talking about... do you have a lot of female followers?' Sandra says, her posture firm, her hand poised just as Magnus had thought it would be, pen just touching the paper as she looks at him.

'Followers?'

'Women who come to watch you in competitions. The beautiful Icelandic women.'

'Well you know... they're not... they're all the same. I have never seen anyone with hair like yours, for example. Never.' Sandra's heart speeds to running. Magnus takes a napkin and re-grips the lid.

'Really. That's so interesting. I suppose I shouldn't put that in the article though.'

Magnus is looking just over Sandra's shoulder at the front of the diner, concentrating desperately. His lips droop apart so that it appears as though his teeth are hanging out of his mouth, limp. He suddenly looks like a walrus, or some kind of large arctic creature. Sandra tries to stay focused. She must win his eyes back. She puts her hand lightly on her neck, something her mother once told her to do.

'So do you find that women in general are impressed with these things that you do?'

'Oh yes, I suppose. But men are also impressed, of course.' Magnus straightens his fingers under the table, stretching his fist and then re-gripping the lid. 'It is nice, isn't it, to do something where people pay attention to you. I suppose. I don't know, I like using my arms and legs.'

'And what are some of the events that you like the most, which are you the best at?'

'Oh, the caber toss, I suppose. And the car haul. Would you excuse me for a moment?'

Magnus rises from the table, keeping the ketchup bottle behind his thigh, but it does not go unnoticed by Sandra. She smiles and removes her fork from the constraints of a tightly rolled napkin where it is mated with a knife and spoon, and spears the quarter tomato which garnishes the platter in front of her. She palms the small salt shaker, gives three vigorous waggles and puts the tomato chunk in her mouth.

Through the small open window to the kitchen at the back of the diner, Magnus can see the quick motions of the cooks, tracks of white streaking against stainless steel. Magnus waves, palm spread, and smiles through the hole. He is spotted by a young man whom Sandra would call a skinny hippie, who looks over his shoulder at the others in the kitchen, and seeing that they are not responding, moves towards the window. Magnus looks at the metal ring hanging from between the boy's nostrils, and thinks of Rögnvaldur, his favorite bull on the farm when he was a young boy. Magnus is suddenly emotional, but reminds himself to keep his feet firmly planted, his knees slightly bent, and his buttocks flexed; he stands at the ready.

'Hello, um, yays, this will not open.'

'Okay, I'll just give you another one, hang on.'

'No – I want this one. I want it open. There is something terribly wrong with it.'

'Listen dude, just take another one.'

The guy goes to the stock shelves, takes a new ketchup bottle, and shakes it energetically as he skips back over to the window.

'Do you want me to open it for you?' the kid says sarcastically.

Magnus takes it and gives him the problem bottle.

'She's going to know it's a different bottle.'

The kid doesn't hear Magnus and walks back into the frenzy. Magnus stares at the bottle. He puts his hand on the lid and slides it open with ease. He stares at it until a waiter approaches him.

'You alright there, pal?'

'Yays, please tell me, where is the toilet?'

The waiter points across the room and Magnus goes quickly through the small door. He ducks as he enters, though he doesn't need to, but sometimes, he has learned, it's better to be excessive than bruised. He goes into a stall and tips the ketchup bottle upside down and waits. Globs of red begin to hit the basin, splashing water onto Magnus. When the bottle is half empty, he screws the lid back on and runs to the door. He continues running through the room until he gets beyond the wall where Sandra can see him, and then walks leisurely to the booth and slides in, believing he is doing it stylishly.

'I also like the keg toss. I have always done very well with that.'

Sandra stares at him, slightly startled. She sees the circles of water on Magnus's trousers and considers several possibilities, none of them very promising. But she reminds herself... different culture, blah blah etc. She writes in her notebook: *Are the kegs empty or full?*

'Oh!' Magnus says, and hands over the ketchup bottle as though he has just remembered.

'Thank you,' Sandra says. She pushes aside the lettuce and globs a pile of ketchup into the space. 'Did you get a different bottle?'

'No. It was just really stuck. Almost like it was melted there, into place. Do you want to see my back?'

Magnus's heart is now for the first time beating undeniably faster. He stares at Sandra, waiting for her reply. Sandra writes down in her notebook: *'Do you want to see my back?' he said.* She is horrified and thrilled.

'Yes, that would be great.'

Magnus stands up and removes his squash shirt in one swoop. At the neighbouring booth, three older women's heads turn simultaneously. One of them loses a mushy lump of bagel out of the gap between her lips. Magnus pulls his arms up over his head and brings them down in a liquid motion to reveal the never-ending passages of grooves on his back. A waiter approaches Magnus from behind with four plates of steak, and passes carefully by, barely brushing his shoulder against Magnus's hip.

'That's great, thanks.' Sandra keeps her face straight and looks down at her pad of paper. 'Great stuff. This will be an easy article to write.' She scribbles onto her pad of paper: *Oh my god!!* She was never one to be impressed by such vile shows of gender-based parades, but there is something in the idea of Magnus: his farmland, his edifying innocence, his altitude. The physique completes what to Sandra can only be called a solid portrait of dense manhood. Magnus makes fists leisurely at his sides, emphasizing his shoulders.

'Magnus Markússon!' an utterly high-pitched voice nearly screams across the diner. A small blond man with furry, light eyebrows comes running over. He is well-built and looks like he would be a good, solid object for Magnus to lift. 'Hvað segirðu gott?'

Magnus stands still and smiling, and extends his arm in a thrust out to the man, who grabs it with both of his. The miniature Icelander has the look of a bouncy-ball, and at one point, his springing motion nearly sends him off the ground.

Sandra's mouth opens slightly. She wants to laugh, and have someone to make eye contact with, to say *Oh come on, what is this clown-show?*

'Sæll!' Magnus says, putting an arm around the guy. 'Hvað heitir þú?'

'Máni Ver Helgasson! Ég er mikill aðdáandi þinn. Ég er frá Akureyri. Ég á heima í New Jersey. Ég ætla að koma og horfa á keppnina á morgun...'

The sounds blend together in Sandra's ear. Every once in a while there is an almost clicking sound in the back of the throat that sounds like it might hurt. She has the feeling of being on a plane and desperately needing to pop the pressure in her ears, or her head will simply explode. She pulls a container which is a combination lipstick holder and mirror out of her purse and snaps it open, looking at her lips. She watches the two men out of the corner of her eye. They are still clasping hands. Must be an Icelandic thing.

'Ég hef búið hér í nokkur ár.'

'Ertu með heimþrá?' Magnus says this last sentence cheerfully, his eyebrows raised. But his eyes look a bit sad, like he is longing for something. Sandra wonders what it is.

'Auðvitað,' the sheep-coloured intruder says.

Blah blah la la la, Sandra thinks, and laughs to herself, admiring her smile in the little mirror. The grin quickly fades as she spots a stiff dark hair growing out of her neck, and pulls at it with her fingers. Then she gives the lipstick a quick pass.

She watches the two standing there touching, and speaking quickly. She finds it ridiculous. But kind of cute. As she snaps the case shut, she sees Magnus leaning down to the man, nearly touching his face with his own cheek.

'Hún er falleg, er það ekki... virkilega falleg,' Magnus says in a half-whisper. His hand is firmly on the shoulder of the lower gentleman, his face a breath's distance away as he slumps his spine over. *She is beautiful, isn't she... really beautiful.*

Sandra watches his movements more carefully. Is it really that loud in here? And it's not as though anyone else can understand what they're saying... they're very close. The mini-Magnus arches his neck back and says close to Magnus's ear, 'Hún er mjög gjaf-vaxta. Gangi pér vel.' *She is very sturdy. Good luck.*

It's probably normal for them. Leaning in like that. Touching. But actually, not really. Sandra figures that the macho element must be present in just about every culture. This is certainly abnormal.

As the words cross her brain like a teleprompter, she sees the face of the tiny man hit Magnus's bare chest. The two embrace; they stand face-to-chest for seconds, holding onto one another's forearms; then, they kiss one another on the cheek.

At this point, she must be honest with herself: several years ago, Sandra made a quiet promise that she wouldn't rationalize horrific truths. After hearing her friends downsize the blatantly horrible behaviours of men, co-workers, and themselves, she promised that she wouldn't turn her life into a pot of psycho-babble narration which validated every stupid turn. And so this is the end of the line; this is where she must get off. As Magnus's arms grasp the knobby shoulder of the little guy, she knows that the boob-staring has been a fascination in size rather than a genuine pursuit.

'Gangi pér vel...' says furry-brow as he turns.

Probably arranging a place to meet later. The two men give a quirky smile as the tiny one walks away. For the love of all things good and holy. It's a parting image that Sandra will now envision in lieu of the little black and white Magnus who still sits in the dark on her bathroom mirror. There is so much tragedy... so much.

'Excuse me, sir, that's not okay at all.' There is a large man standing next to Magnus, whom Magnus can only identify as being very very dark seeming. He has a thick brow which never separates and he stands with his arms crossed and his eyes shining, his apron spotted in thick grease.

'Take a seat, pal,' the waiter says, 'and put that little racquetball shirt back on yourself.' If a passerby were to look inside the diner from the street, the waiter would look like Magnus's bastard son, robust but still a full foot shorter than Magnus, who does not tilt his head downward when he speaks, but merely lowers his eyes.

'I am sorry,' Magnus says tenderly, 'I am sitting down now.' Sandra now notices how gentle he is. She should have seen it sooner. The soft, pastel giant.

'Well what are the chances of that!' Sandra says. She has never been able to resist using her gay-man voice when she meets one. It's awful, and she's been persistently trying to stop. It's high-pitched and goes up and down in unnatural waves. She looks directly at Magnus, not wanting to make him feel bad. She has to accept him. God only knows what they might do with him in Iceland.

'It's so strange, I run into Icelanders all over the world. All over. He is so sweet.'

'He seems very sweet,' Sandra says. She nearly has to physically restrain herself from rolling her eyes.

'Or maybe sweet isn't the word... I don't know, because sweet and cute in Icelandic are the same word,' Magnus says.

'Mmm-hm.'

There is silence. Magnus sits smiling, the sounds of home in his mind, and the satisfaction of his growing fan base. Sandra puts her head on her hand, and looks out the window. She knows that this slumping dissatisfaction is date behavior and not particularly professional, but Magnus wouldn't possibly differentiate between the two, and she really can't help it.

'You're tired,' Magnus says, still feeling a bit giddy. Sandra tries desperately to perk up; she doesn't want to hurt Magnus's feelings with her own depression. After all, he's worth his weight in fish. 'Maybe we should continue this elsewhere,' he says. Magnus feels light and unstoppable. Tomorrow will be a great day, and tonight, with any luck, he will conquer the west.

Sandra looks up at him with a sloppy face, but manages to produce a sappy smile. She wishes she were back in her bathroom, brushing her teeth and looking at the mute Magnus in black and white, and wondering what it would be like to stand next to him. If this happens one more time, she should move out of New York.

'Maybe we should go back to my hotel and continue the interview, and maybe get a drink at the bar there.' Magnus almost stops there, but feels a certain power and boldness, and as he doesn't have much time left, he decides he will go full throttle. He feels now that this evening is meant to happen, that nothing will stop the fates. 'I like to have a release before the competitions.'

I bet you do, Sandra thinks, and then is glad she didn't say it aloud, not because it is rude but because out of any woman in this situation, she figures at least 70% of them would have thought that exact sentence. But self-flagellation must wait for after the diner. But what is he asking for?

Magnus stares one last time at her breasts. He wonders what they look like unsupported. And then supported in his hands. And then other things. He wonders exactly how heavy she is.

He continues on. 'My hotel room is so nice. One of the nicest I've seen. And I've been all over the world.'

'So have I,' Sandra replies, staring, eyebrows raised, at Magnus.

'Of course. But I bet you have not seen a hotel room like this.

And on the eighth floor there is a rotating bar. It's fun. We can talk more there, and you can write a really good story.'

Sandra says nothing, but is remarkably confused. Generally in any interpersonal situation, especially surrounding work, her mind would be battling through various scenarios and explanations for a person's behaviour. At this moment, she can't think of anything. Except that Magnus could be speaking an exact truth: that he needs a good and proper release before the competition.

Magnus notes the change in Sandra's expression. Thank god the ketchup bottle didn't ruin him. Magnus feels his own gravity successfully hauling in Sandra. Sandra doesn't know what is going on, but she figures she should go with the flow. You take what you can get.

'I will be gentle,' Magnus says.

'Okay. Thank you.' It's all she can think to say. At this point it probably doesn't matter. In the end it may be a sad story to tell, Sandra thinks, and she may not be able to bring him around to the family, or walk for a week afterward, but you do what you can. She'll have to write the story tomorrow morning.

YOU CANNOT ESCAPE IT, YOU CAN ONLY HOPE TO CONTAIN IT

Joshua Isard

YOU CANNOT ESCAPE IT,
YOU CAN ONLY HOPE TO CONTAIN IT

Joshua Isard

MATT, WEARING ONLY A damp towel wrapped nearly twice around his waist, dived across the living room of his London flat to answer the phone before the voice mail picked up.

'Hullo,' he said, out of breath.

'Hello boychek!' an unexpected American woman exclaimed.

'Hi Mom,' Matt said.

'Matthew, you're out of breath,' his mother panicked, 'what's the matter?'

'Nothing Mom,' he answered, 'I was expecting someone else, that's all. I just stepped out of the shower.'

'You wouldn't run out of energy if you ate more, honey. I worry about you with that skinny body.'

'I'm not anaemic, Mom, just thin. I run a lot.'

'You'll have to find yourself a nice Jewish girl to make you lots of food.'

'Right Mom. Look, I'm sorry, but I'm getting ready to go out, I don't have a lot of time to talk right now.'

'Oh, that's okay, your Bubby is over the house and I just wanted to call for a minute while she's here. We're so proud of our boy going to college for a whole year in England!'

'Hi Bubby.'

'He says "Hi!"' Matt's mother screamed across her kitchen without moving the receiver away from her mouth. 'What? I don't know? Maybe. Matthew, who are you going out with?'

'This girl I met a few days ago. I thought she may have been calling from a broken tube station or something –'

'He's got a date!' Matt had to pull the phone away from his ear as the women in his family became more excited about the night than he was. His grandmother yelled in the background, 'What's her name!'

'Tell Bubby her name's Annette.'

'Oooohh Matt!' His mother was as giddy as his younger sister had been when she found out her friend's friend had once thought she'd seen a member of *NSYNC in the mall. Matt sighed, invaded by apathy. The family expected him to find a nice Jewish girl, even while living in a country with a cross on its flag. Soon enough, he would have to tell all.

'Now Matthew,' his grandmother said after grabbing another phone on the same line, 'is this girl from a nice family? The Jewish women in Britain have to be raised well enough for my number one grandson.'

'She's not British, actually' Matt said.

'Oh,' both women said at once. 'Well,' his mother asked, 'is she Scottish?'

Matthew swallowed hard, knowing it would be better to be up front with his family about this. After all, he thought, they are reasonable, modern people, though perhaps geopolitically misguided. His mother the Registered Nurse, and his grandmother the most frequent traveller on the road from North Jersey to Atlantic City – they should both be accepting.

'She's German, actually.'

Matthew was amazed how polite an operator with an English accent sounded, even while telling him the connection had been lost, and to please try again.

* * *

'Wow, Annette, you sure look nice tonight!'

'I do not like this skirt you gave me.'

'Like I told you, men aren't impressed by dirty blue jeans and concert T-shirts. You have to look posh.'

'I am sorry Vicky, but I forget the way the English tell others to go away.'

'Sod off?'

'Yes. That was it. Sod off, Vicky.'

The two flat mates smiled, and Annette began to describe her date for the evening.

'When we met at the Tate he was very sweet. His friends laugh at him while we talked but he paid attention to me. He explained paintings to me I had not ever seen.'

'I can't believe he chatted you up at an art museum. At least you found someone else who likes that stuff.'

'It is very good, Vicky. You should look some time.'

Vicky laughed off the comment, not even wanting to waste time thinking about such a place.

'Annette, can I help you with your make-up?'

'I do not wear make up often. Do you think that I should?'

'You want to impress him, right? You should look your best on the first date.'

'But it is not like me.'

'It's not you, but it's for him.'

Annette grudgingly agreed, never having been on a date in the Anglo world. The two made their way into the bathroom where Vicky sorted through her large bins of cosmetics. *Boots* should have sent her a personal 'thank you' for helping them through tough economic times.

'When is he showing up?' Vicky began, deciding between the final two mascara candidates, 'I want to meet this bloke.'

'We are meeting at South Kensington. I did not want him here yet.'

'Okay,' Vicky said, not wanting to question how German women do things, 'best to keep some control in the beginning.'

'Yes, that is right.'

'So,' Vicky asked, 'where are you going?'

'Matthew said he is aware of a good French restaurant near the V & A museum.'

'Oh! That is so sweet! Wine, music, he's so nice! I'm glad you met a good English man, not some bastard who doesn't know how to treat a woman. Or worse, one of those cheap Americans who come here and assume women'll drop their trousers at an accent. One time at a pub with some of my friends from Uni I met these boys from the States – wouldn't even buy us drinks! Just assumed we'd go back to theirs. Idiots.'

'Akt-oo-al-ly,' Annette said, having trouble with the polysyllabic word and sounding it out phonetically, 'he is not English.' Vicky quickly considered where he could be from, while thickening her flat mate's lashes. New Zealand? Not eating French food. Irish? Not if he wasn't laughing at the Tate. Australian? Not if he was in the Tate. Vicky's jaw dropped, knowing just before Annette revealed it, the only English speaking national who would take his German date to a French restaurant. 'He is from New Jersey,' Annette said.

* * *

Matt strolled to the Baker Street tube stop. He took care to avoid any possibility of dirt getting on his khakis, which stained easily. His blue oxford shirt never caused him any problems.

Near the entrance Matt ran into his flat mate, and fellow seditious colonial, Dave, coming home from a long Friday afternoon at happy hour. Matt would have preferred a short greeting with minimal breaking of strides, but Dave wanted someone to spill his alcoholic giddiness on.

'Oy!' Dave yawped, trying hard to sound more English. Despite the usually valid maxim when in Rome, the use of some English words in an American accent sounds ridiculous. Not knowing instinctively which letters to omit in British slang, Dave sounded out every syllable, his sentences holding the grace of a first time ice skater trying a triple toe-loop. 'Hey there, mate!'

'Hi Dave. Did you go to the bars today?'

'Aye, aye. I'm a bit elephants now, if you know what I mean.'

'I know, Dave. Look, I have to run, sorry man.'

'Oh, right, the big date tonight.'

'Yeah. I've got to meet her at Tottenham Court, so, you know, time to ru–'

'Say, is this the German bird?' When Dave pronounced a hard 'r' in bird it sounded as if he only said the word to impress the Englishmen around him with his cultured vocabulary. Often, the local Londoners got a laugh out of his efforts.

'Yes. Annette.'

'You said she wore combat boots when you met her, right,' Dave said with the hint of a laugh in his voice.

'No. No, she had these black boots and dark blue jeans, not, like, five inch thick soles and metal buckles or anything. She looked a little neo-punk, that's all.'

'Oh, man!' Dave yelped, 'You have some serious iron bollocks taking this one out. A Jew and a German in this day and age. The last taboo. Where are you taking her?'

'This French place near the V & A museum.'

'Ha!' Dave couldn't hold his laughter as mental images of a six foot tall, shit-kicking woman dressed in black leather sat across the table from Gap-ad-Matt. With accordion music in the background. 'You have a good time, Matt,' he said through his laughter.

'What? What are you laughing at? Why is this such a big deal?'

'How'd you pick up a German girl at an art museum? That takes skill.'

'I was explaining something about a Rothko painting to her and –'

'Isn't he the guy on the cover of your coffee table book?'

'Yeah.'

'The one with the pictures from Jewish artists.'

'Oh my god, Dave, why does this matter?'

Dave began buckling at the knees as laughter overcame him. 'Oh, it's just the complete lack of irony, that's all.' He patted his friend on the back, and before leaving grabbed Matt's gold, six-pointed star which had fallen out of his shirt. 'Better put this one away. Button up a bit more.' Dave left, walking in rhythm with his own laughter.

'Fucking hell,' Matt said aloud to himself. 'How weird can this possibly be? We're just two people that get along well with each other. I guess.'

Matt took the escalator down to get on the tube, wondering just what he was missing about the differences between the national identities of he and his date. Despite a recent history of war and destruction, breeding the natural hatred between the peoples, they were human beings. He tried to justify their connection by thinking about how well most people adapt to new situations.

Like Dave in England.

A slight tremor of panic ran down his back.

He decided their cultures might not make the best conversation that evening.

* * *

They met at the South Kensington tube station, each with a slight trepidation stemming from their friend's and family's responses to the unusual union of traditional enemies. Matt gave Annette a light, friendly hug and she responded with a kiss for both of his cheeks. She paused for a moment, thinking she had felt the vibration of teeth chattering when she put her lips to Matt's face, but shrugged it off.

What happened on the outside:

'You look wonderful tonight, Annette.'

'Thank you. My flat mate helped me to dress. I do not usually wear skirts.'

'Don't worry, you look great.'

He took her arm in his. She grabbed on tightly. They began walking towards the restaurant.

What happened on the inside:

Matt noticed that even with his thick soled Doc Marten's, Annette trumped his six foot tall, slim frame. When they'd met he held a height advantage, but now she wore heels, making her about an inch taller than him. Her shirt wrapped tightly around her full upper body, and her skirt did nothing to hide her thick, but not disproportionate, lower body. He felt more like the pitiful but sweet best friend than the chivalrous man out to entertain a woman.

Annette noticed a mild tremor in Matt's hand while he held hers. She did not connect it with the possibility that she was twice the size of any of Matt's previous girlfriends in America, all in a silent struggle to be the smallest most fragile creature on the planet, but instead, remembering what her lips felt beneath his cheek, drew some of the most extreme solutions right away. He was a smoker who had given up for the night to look classier. He was a drug user (one of the first English language movies Annette had ever seen was *The Basketball Diaries*) trying to quit and start a normal life with a nice girl. He had never been on a date before and was trying hard to hold himself together. But that's where she stopped herself, realizing that other things in his life beside this date could agitate his nerves.

Like bombs.

The couple passed by the Victoria and Albert Museum on their way to the restaurant, and Matt promptly noticed the large pieces of stone missing from the structure's outer walls; damage he knew resulted from the Nazi bombing of London during World War II. Annette saw him staring for an unusually long time at the museum, and stopped to take a closer look herself.

'What do you look at?' she asked sweetly.

'Oh,' Matt said, happy to be off the so-how-are-you-doing part of the date in only a few minutes. 'The museum, there, it has damage on its walls.'

'Where?' she enquired, not seeing any broken stone through the crepuscular light.

'Right there,' Matt said, inching closer to her so she could follow his finger pointing out the chipped bricks. He took pride in finding a way to get nearly cheek-to-cheek with a girl while still in the single digit minutes of date number one.

'I see,' she said, not knowing exactly what she saw. They caught each other's eyes and smiled, faces about two inches from one another. Matt considered kissing her right there, relying on the stories he had heard about how open European women were about sex. Annette wanted him to kiss her, but also hoped he would live up to the American gentleman image she had constructed for him out of popular romantic comedies with German subtitles.

After a few seconds of wavering between getting to the point and saving the best for last, Annette asked what had happened to the museum. She thought his explanation would give them a few more moments in that close, near embrace.

But Matt stumbled backwards as he almost told his nice date that her country had spent a few years bombing the hell out of the city which basically stood as the last bastion between a sadistic dictator and freedom as they knew it. It didn't take the higher levels of reasoning to place that firmly in the category of ways-to-get-off-to-a-bad-start.

'Umm, I don't really know what happened,' he said. 'Just interesting, isn't it?'

'I think, yes. We can maybe find out on one of these... pieces of writing here. Near the gates.'

'We don't have time to read the plaques,' he said, checking his watch though he knew full well they were on time, 'we're running a bit late. Come on,' he said, trying to make himself look in control again, taking her arm in his. Her heel scraped against the ground as he tugged her along.

Matt, despite a large smile, confused Annette by remaining taciturn during the rest of their walk towards the restaurant. She wondered if the skirt and make-up Vicky had forced on her made Matt nervous. Annette thought the German equivalent of 'if it ain't broke...'

Matt asked himself why he wouldn't just give the girl the facts, there was no need for bloody details. Then Matt thought of the many ways he would later hurt Dave for giving him such a 'stupid American' mentality.

* * *

A portly, heavily made up French woman with grey streaks in her black hair greeted Matt and his date at the door of the sparsely furnished restaurant. She led them to a table made to look like century old wood, but with an overt finish to it, robbing the effect like a £100 pair of pre-ripped jeans.

They ordered a bottle of wine, and once left alone looked at each other over the tall burning candle in the center of the table. Matt began to sink into the first moment outside the intolerant world, but Annette's gaze moved to the right of his head, and when he asked what was wrong she covertly pointed to the table behind him. A family of four sat there, enjoying their main course, without a distinguishing characteristic except that the two young boys and their father had small, dark red skullcaps atop their thick, curly hair.

'The little hats make me smile,' Annette whispered.

'What, the yarmulkes?' Matt replied.

'Is that what they are called?'

'Uh, yeah.'

'They are cute.'

Cute, Matt thought. It was one thing for Jews to use self deprecating humour, but for others it crossed the line.

'Why are you so interested?' Matt asked.

'We do not have many Jewish people in Germany.'

Gee, wonder why that is, Matt thought, but managed to keep it inside.

He took a quick look back at the kipah wearing boys and reconsidered his sentiments. Annette didn't know how uncomfortable her little laugh made him, and she hadn't exactly called for the family's destruction on account of strange headwear. Really, the things did look a bit ridiculous some times. Especially pinned to large, fluffy, Jewish hair styles, like those two boys wore. Poor kids.

The wine arrived, which pleased Annette who hoped it would take away some of the strange anxiety hanging around her date like fog on the London streets. He had been so confident at the museum, paying such close attention to their conversation, and to her in general. Maybe he hadn't expected her to look so... normal, Annette thought.

She wanted to help him regain the self assuredness that so attracted her in front of the canvasses, so she put him on familiar ground by asking about his job.

'Well, I'm a student, actually.' Matt proudly described his program of international business. 'Six years of University and I'll have my MBA. And they get me experience here, so I won't lose a step to the people working while I study.'

For a few moments he felt comfortable. His job was to erase, or seemingly erase, borders, to make transition easier. After years of training for major corporate transactions across borders, seas, and oceans, a date with a girl who spoke his own language began to seem routine.

Annette felt better too while her date regained some of his composure as he talked. She tried to move the conversation from the work to family, because she thought nothing could be easier to talk about.

'Where does your family come from?' Annette asked.

'We're all from New Jersey.'

'No, I meant, where do they start?'

'You mean where they came from before America?'

'Yes.'

'They emigrated... went to America... in the Thirties and Forties.'

'From where did they come to America?'

Poland. 'Russia.' Not much better. The shame is endless. Don't ask why, Matt thought, please don't ask why, we've already dodged this whole thing once.

'Okay,' Annette said, now thinking anything would agitate the nerves of this guy. She looked at her watch for the first time that night. 'What does your mother and father work as?'

The progression of discourse on to his parents in medicine and her parents in real estate provided an ephemeral bubble of relief.

* * *

After benign conversation over main courses covering the significant histories of their lives, sans any mention of past significant others which had to be reserved for a time more conducive to self-deprecation, Matt and Annette decided to split a dessert before going on their way.

The French woman brought them a large bowl of fruits and cream, but accidentally dropped Matt's spoon while setting new utensils. Matt quickly picked the spoon up off the floor and handed it to the waitress. He received another one and began an attack on the sweet dessert, but stopped as he saw Annette gaping at his chest. Well aware of the absence of any pectoral muscles, and the terribly thin, straggly hair which insisted upon growing from his body, Matt wished he had taken Dave's advice to button up more.

Annette looked, could not pull herself away from, the sight of Matt's Jewish star which had fallen out of his shirt. It explained all his odd behavior through the evening. Glowing bright white while reflecting the candle's flame, the star rested comfortably, and obviously, against Matt's blue shirt.

'Oh,' Matt stumbled, shoving the amulet back into his shirt and buttoning up one more level.

'I did not know you are Jewish.'

'Um, yeah,' Matt said, 'I'm not observant, really, it's just... my family...'

'It is okay. That thing does not matter to me.'

'But... what about...' Matt pointed over his shoulder at the Hebraic quartet.

'That means nothing. If you saw a man wearing lederhosen in Trafalgar Square you would think it is silly. Yes?'

Matt had to agree. Annette leaned over the table and gently removed the star again, holding it gently in her hand, then looking up at Matt. 'Do you have a funny hat too?' she asked.

* * *

Annette walked into her flat, closed the door behind herself, and then leaned against it in satisfaction. Vicky had waited for her with the loyalist of companions, Mr Cadbury. 'Well?' Vicky demanded from the couch, 'is he here?'

'No, Vicky.'

'Then you saw his flat?'

'No.'

'What a gentleman,' Vicky sarcastically mumbled to herself, 'or a complete muppet.'

Annette walked into the living room and sat with Vicky. She went through the date from start to finish, from meeting at the tube stop, to the museum (which the English woman felt an obligation to explain nicely), to every detail about the restaurant memorable through the still effective wine. It took an entire repeated episode of *Graham Norton* to complete the story.

'So you found yourself an American Jew,' Vicky said, 'the world never ceases to amaze me. I suppose that's the end of that.'

'No,' Annette said, 'we will meet next week again.'

'Don't you think that's a bit odd, though?'

'No.'

'Well, next time we'll make you up good and proper for the future business tycoon.'

'I do not think so, Vicky. Perhaps I will be more me on the next time.'

* * *

Matt slumped down next to Dave on their sofa, stained by five brands of beer thus far in their tenancy. The first of two *South Park* episodes had just come on TV.

'How was your night?' Dave asked.

'Er… all right.'

'Shag the German bird? Win one for your people?'

'No, Dave, I didn't.'

'Snog her?'

'No. Just walked her home, set up another date.'

'Sounds like a boring night.'

Dave offered Matt a can of John Smith ale, an offer quickly accepted. The two then proceeded to disengage their minds from reality. After the first episode and one beer Matt said he wanted to go to sleep.

'All right,' Dave said, 'I'll see you tomorrow.'

Matt brushed his teeth, changed his clothes, and was ready to close his door for the evening when Dave called out to him.

'What, Dave?'

'Forgot to tell you. Your mum phoned, said she was sorry for hanging up on you, and that she didn't get your joke right away. Don't know what that means, but I promised I'd tell you.'

Matt nodded, closed his door, and turned off the light.

THE BIRD

Aimee Chalmers

THE BIRD

Aimee Chalmers

WHEN YOU WERE wee you used to hide under the table, listening to other folk talking. Trying to make out what was going on. You never had much to say for yourself and nobody asked for your opinion.

So, here you are now, twenty three years old, living in a foreign land, still listening to other folk talking. In Greek. Trying to make out what's going on. Not much to say for yourself. Nobody interested in your opinion.

Maybe it's something about you.

You're standing in the bathroom, in front of the mirror. It's a nice bathroom, a very good size for a one-bedroom flat. Luckily, as it turns out.

You've just stepped out of the shower. The bath towel is wrapped round your body. Your reflection glowers at you. You lean forward, clench your teeth, stretch your lips sideways, bare all. Look at your teeth rather than into your eyes. Then look away, from what could be either a grimace or a false smile.

Teeth. You squeeze the tube carefully, from the bottom. Half an inch is plenty. Make it last.

The toothpaste is from the health food shop. You bought it before you left home, so you must have had it for... four weeks, three days. Roughly. Maybe. But maybe you just started using it when you got here. Yes. So that's four weeks. Still, it's lasting well.

It tastes like toothpaste used to, no carboxymethyl-cellulose sodium, or sodium lauryl sulphate or colloidal anhydrous silica or anything like that in it. You don't think so, anyway. You see the back of the tube in the mirror. Something makes you stop, look at it.

It's indecipherable. You think it's written in Greek.

You're shocked. You know you bought it at home.

But it's not Greek, it's just the reflection, backwards.

Okay. Take yourself in hand. Screw the top off.

You wince.

You lift the brush to your mouth. Lips apart, teeth tight together. You always have the same routine. It's familiar. Front upper, front lower.

A bird flies in. This is a big bird, not your ordinary wee spuggie that's got confused, taken a wrong turn and flown in the window accidentally. And this one flew in the door. Bold as brass, a kamikaze bird.

You might have called out if your mouth wasn't full of toothpaste and brush. Your brushing hand freezes just for a second. And your eyes open wide, you can see that in the mirror. Then your expression begins to reflect the questions tumbling inside your head. These lines appear on your forehead. A frown.

Something makes you carry on as normal. In fact, if anything, you probably give *front upper, front lower* extra time as you try to puzzle it out.

You could say it's your own fault for leaving the bathroom door open, but that's not the point really. Living on your own, there's no need to shut yourself in. And if you leave the bathroom door open you can hear if someone rings the front door bell. Not that anyone ever does.

And you can escape if you need to, from… spiders, cockroaches. The spiders aren't so bad. Familiar looking. But you don't like the cockroaches. You never come into the bathroom at night without your slippers on, just in case the cockroaches are on the march. You wouldn't want to feel one of them wriggling under you. No. They have a very thick skin… thick shell, you mean.

You glance down at your feet. Of course you have your slippers on.

The bird doesn't seem to be distressed at all. It's hovering quietly behind you, slightly to the window side. You wonder whether you should open the window. But you don't want to make any sudden movements, and anyway you are in the middle of cleaning your teeth.

Front upper right, front upper left.

Strange that the bird should fly in today though, the very day you wondered about closing the bathroom door.

You think it's probably about the size of a parrot. But then, not being an expert on birds, especially foreign ones, what would you know? It's not brightly coloured though. It's more subtle, you can see that. Feathers shimmer like the dim reflection of a rainbow on Rescobie Loch on a dull day. Ghostly iridescent colours that tease your eyes, that change before your brain can put a name to them.

A moving picture on the surface of the mirror, plays like a memory on a screen.

The harbour, the sun setting in that haste you can't quite get used to, that plunge into a negative. So unlike the slow summer twilights of home, that linger.

A bicycle parked beside a yacht. Silhouetted against the sea. An interesting juxtaposition.

You went to take a photograph. A man climbing from a yacht. Tanned, healthy looking, fit. His smile.

You shake your head, slowly from side to side. The image fades.

Your body is angled straight ahead, but you've focussed your eyes to the left. Or does that mean it's the right? A mirror image, remember. You feel panic rising in your chest. Which hand do you write with? Your right. The one you're holding your toothbrush in. So the bird is on your left.

You look at your hands, feel fluttering in your chest.

You try again. You're looking at the mirror... the bird is behind you. Your eyes jump from side to side as your brain tries to catch up. You try to keep calm, can't quite remember something...

Front lower right, front lower left.

Behind you. That's it, isn't it. It's because it's all behind you. If you were to turn round, the bird would be on your right. That's the explanation. You feel better. It's all behind you.

You don't like to stare at the bird, not even in the mirror. It seems perfectly happy. You wouldn't want to antagonise it. It probably has as much right to be here as you do.

You change position, not so much as the bird would notice, but enough to get a better impression from the corner of your eye. The bird seems at ease, not put out at all.

Okay. Now open up. Back upper right, back upper left, back upper front. That's how you normally do them.

It seems to hover effortlessly. You can hear a faint whirr of wings but you can't see them. No need to make a fuss then. Ignore it.

You relax a little, wonder if this is maybe an auspicious moment. Something to do with the way your stars are aligned, which planet is in opposition to which, whether the moon is linking with your two rulers, or where your sun is focused. But well, you were never confident in what horoscopes said.

Trouble is, there's always more than one interpretation, always more than one way to read the omens. So you don't really know.

It's certainly lucky that the bathroom's a decent size. But even so, there isn't that much room for a bird.

Back lower right, back lower left. Back lower front. That's the awkward bit, when you have to turn the toothbrush perpendicular. But it's important. It's where bits of food get stuck.

There. You know you can't avoid this any more.

You spit into the basin. You think that you deserve privacy for some things. You throw the bird a vaguely resentful look, which is ignored.

Time for the rinse. You turn the tap on, run water over your toothbrush, turn it off again. You know not to waste water.

A fairly peremptory once-all-over with the clean brush. Another spit, this time done more decorously. You grimace in the mirror, teeth clenched. They're clean. You inspect the front filling that the dentist gave you on your last visit. Remarkable how invisible something like that can be. You, and the dentist are probably the only two people in the world who know about that.

There's an audible change to the fluttering behind your head. The bird is on your right now. You can see the wings. Very graceful, considering the restricted circumstances.

The bird perches on the top of the cane shelf unit you bought at the market last week. Or was it the week before? The time goes by so quickly. Anyway, it was the same day you bought the pottery dish from Makrinitsa and the hand carved wooden spoon.

You're glad you chose the cane unit. Chrome wouldn't have looked so natural for a perch.

You rinse the toothbrush, shake it, put it back in the rack. As the brush-head jolts on the frame, a thought strikes you. You wonder if somebody's watching. You glance in the mirror, towards the window. The door. A hidden camera? Somebody trying to get a laugh at you, catch you out.

Well, the best way to deal with that is to pretend you haven't noticed. You straighten your back, half fill a tumbler of water, and screw that tap off tightly again. You squish a mouthful of water backwards and forwards through your teeth. Spit out. Amazing how you can get used to things.

You put the top on the toothpaste. You'll need to get some more in a few weeks time. You hope you can get it here.

You've forgotten to rinse the sink. You turn the tap on again, swirl water round the sink with the cloth you keep just for that purpose. Turn the tap off quickly again. It's very important to save water, to live like local people. You take your responsibilities seriously.

There, that'll do.

You hesitate briefly, decide what to do. You turn, give the bird a quick wee nod and excuse yourself as you go. It preens itself. You made the right decision.

You wonder whether you should shut the door. No, leave it.

You'll have to go back into the bedroom.

You push gently at the door, peer round, tiptoe to the side of the bed where your clothes are lying discarded. That wasn't like you at all, to leave clothes on the floor. You're normally very tidy.

You pick things up, sort them. Quietly.

But there's no sign of movement from the bed. The guy is inert. He's almost totally covered by the sheet, but you can see muscular calves sticking out at one end, his dark straight black hair at the other. God, it looks oily. You didn't notice that last night. The pillowcase...

He's lying face down, leaning on an arm. You can't quite remember what his face looked like. You lean over to try to see it and think he's paler than he was last night.

The smile. White teeth. That's what you remember. And he had an athletic body. Was athletic.

You wonder how old he was. Late thirties? You reckon he was probably early forties.

The yacht was called *Ariadne*. It wasn't grand, quite small actually, but still must have been worth a bit of money. And was trim, beautifully maintained. He'd taken you on board, shown you round.

You'd had an ouzo on deck. Maybe a few.

With your attempt at Greek and his attempt to speak English, it was amazing how much... how you'd managed...

Maybe you didn't learn that much about him.

You went together to a nightclub at the town beach, but can't remember how you got there. Or here.

You resent him lying in your bed. You want to pull the sheet off, tell him to *fuck off* but you're not sure how he'd take it. And you can't remember his name. You're really not sure whether he's breathing or not. You can't see any movement.

Two problems, then. A bird in the bathroom, a very still nameless yachtsman in the bedroom. You can't stand this.

You decide to go for a walk, even though it's early. You dress quickly, leave the bedroom and the bathroom doors open.

It's so quiet in the empty streets that your footsteps echo. You look behind to see who is following. But you might be the only person left in the world.

You pause down at the harbour, the quay where the locals anchor their fishing boats. The water laps quietly against them. A soft breeze carries the troubled sound of metal on wood across from the marina where the yachts are moored.

The sun is low in the sky. The bright play of light on water makes your eyes uncomfortable. You blink, blink. Squeeze eyes tight. Blink.

The air is cool.

A REGIME CHANGE OF THE HEART

Brian D. Algra

A REGIME CHANGE OF THE HEART

Brian D. Algra

AP – Baghdad, Iraq 20-3-03: Amanda Lenville followed the servingman down into the dining chamber and, smoothing her ankle-length abaaya over her hips, took the seat she was offered.

She studied the room around her.

What was going on with its goofy ambience? The subdued lighting, she was willing to grant, was probably a permanent feature, designed to enhance the play of shadow over its plaster-work ceilings and antiquity-laden alcoves. But the strains of soft Sinatra, stealing from the ceiling speakers? The scented candles and rose-petal placemats? The olives and oysters on gold-leafed plates, and the bottle of cold Cristal, laid out on ice?

Not even President Clinton had been able to contrive such a ludicrous scene for their meetings. In fact, Amanda mused, were it not for the Uzi-toting guards stationed at each corner of the table, the whole thing would read like a premise for some cheap romance novel, some ridiculous story of lust and love amidst the splendors of Arabia.

She scoffed at the comparison. If this was set to be a bodice-ripping fairy tale, then where was the fair Prince Charming who'd invited her here? Amanda had done everything he'd requested: she had ditched her cameraman and dispensed with her tape recorder, and she'd driven – alone – to Radwaniyah at 4am, defying every network rule she knew of in order to accommodate his 'busy schedule.'

All that, and he couldn't even show up on time! She looked at the table again and frowned. Any sort of preferment he'd hoped to gain from this display of Middle Eastern daddy-macking was sure to be wasted by his lack of punctuality.

'I'm nothing,' Amanda bitched internally, 'if not a professional, and I'm entitled to expect the same of those with whom I work.' She slurped up the nearest oyster with a calculated lack of tact. 'I don't care how important this assignment is. If he thinks of me as some decadent Western Everywoman, some common Tupperware trollop who can be kept waiting, plied with fine food and wine into acquiescence to his bidding, he's got another thing coming!'

Having lathered herself into this decidedly unprofessional state of mind, Amanda dug into her briefcase, resolving to brush up on what, in the service of journalistic impartiality, she'd tried for two long weeks to forget. The document she drew out – a dossier prepared by her pro-war editors in Atlanta – provided a damning survey of her meal companion's most monstrous abuses of power.

'Saddam Hussein,' it read, 'The Butcher of Baghdad.' The so-called 'elected President' of Iraq and a self-declared champion of pan-Arabism, Hussein is, in actuality, a vicious dictator who rules by terror alone. Within the past fifteen years, this dangerous megalomaniac has – by way of example – assassinated, widowed or orphaned no fewer than twelve members of his own family. He has arranged for the arrest and eventual execution of tens of thousands of Iraqi innocents. He has utilized revenue from illicit Syrian oil sales to develop weapons of mass destruction (WMDs), and has repeatedly violated international protocols by deploying said weapons – specifically, Sarin and mustard gases – against Iranian soldiers and domestic Kurdish civilians during conflicts in the 1980s and 90s. Hussein's more personal abuses are nearly as outrageous. A notorious Epicurean, he has forced his people to starve while he lives with the luxury of twenty Presidential Palaces, two hundred European sports cars, a thousand well-stocked bars, an untold number of mistresses, and two... two...'

Amanda's train of thought was interrupted by the arrival of a tall and well-dressed man at the table: Saddam, the man himself, had appeared at last. She looked down at his shining Bruno Magli shoes. She examined his exquisitely-tailored Savile Row suit. She scanned up to his powerful shoulders, to the flowing moustache which framed his wry silent mouth. And then, at last, her eyes met his and – in a moment that would change her life forever – lost themselves, unaccountably, irrevocably, in the fortified underground bunkers of his gaze. Unable to finish reading the dossier, Amanda sighed the rest of the sentence to herself.

'...And two... two... rapturously beautiful brown eyes.'

2

Amanda had never experienced such a moment before. Gripped by the gaze of this powerful man, every particle of her pent-up prejudice, every atom of her accumulated irritation, was split apart in a massive chain reaction of desire. The radiological intensity of Saddam's scrutiny seemed to burn through her clothes, to scorch her naked flesh beneath, to render her very being transparent to his piercing perception.

And then he spoke.

'Good morning, Miss Lenville. And thank you for agreeing to this private conference. Allow me to say that you appear even more alluring in person – and in the traditional costume of our country – than you do on television.'

Amanda usually preferred 'Ms', but under the circumstances she knew she lacked all power to retort. His voice – low and sonorous, infused with Eastern exoticism – enthralled her now.

She closed her eyes as she absorbed its seductive tones. Her insides quivered in concert with its clefs and crescendos; her spinal cord conducted its choruses down to the triangular tuning fork of her pudendum. Its pitch was pure coitus: any more of it, she felt, and her garters would snap at its wielder's whim. The window to her sex and soul would be shattered, and together, like looters in love's service, she and Saddam Hussein would pillage the products contained within.

Only once these sinuous waves of speech had passed from her system did Amanda awake, with a shot, to the absurdity of her situation. 'Me and Saddam Hussein!' she echoed, as precarious with her grammar as she was with her emotions. 'How can I even be thinking such a thing?'

How indeed, raced her mind, could this be happening to her – to *her*, Amanda Lenville, of all people? Hadn't she spent a lifetime rejecting feelings like these?

Had she not, at eighteen, when her chestnut hair and rousing knockers gained her the title of prom queen, taken the mic and informed her horrified classmates that 'true love' was a tool of masculinist oppression – a marketing creation designed to thwart the claim of Woman to a proper share in society? And had she not – in college and since – accepted as gospel the words of her gender theory professor: 'Who controls sex, controls the future?'

She had stuck to these creeds – stuck to them and prospered, even as her friends around her sold themselves away to manufactured, Someday-My-Soulmate-Will-Come fantasies of princes, forbidden passion and Paris in the spring.

It hadn't always been easy, this road less travelled by: her ambitions had landed her in more than a few unpalatable positions (Wolf Blitzer, for one, would never look the same to her again). But whenever she found she was losing her way, she'd needed only think of those same old friends out there – married, mortgaged and minivanning their 1.6 to school each morning – for reassurance that her choices were the right ones. She was the 'Baghdad Bombshell' for Pete's sake: a 21st-century Scud Stud, and CNN's celebrated bearer of 'Hard-Hitting News from the Mouth of a Babe.' She'd earned that tagline, and she'd gotten this interview, because she knew what her friends refused to acknowledge: that love was a commodity like any other, to be bought and sold to best advantage.

This was so, she insisted to herself. It had always been so! But then why was she so struck by this man across the table, by his eyes, by the timbre of his voice? She had been prepared for almost anything, coming here – any spurious twist of words, any propaganda technique, even any physical threat to her person, if it came to that. But for Saddam to be so, well... *disarming*? This, she managed to chuckle, was beyond anyone's expectations.

In any case, Amanda reflected, whether by stratagem or just some strange stroke of luck, Saddam had seized the upper hand. He had her feeling helpless and unallied, as though he were pointing a loaded Kalashnikov straight at her loins, and demanding that she surrender them to inspection. Well, she couldn't stand for it: she'd simply have to will herself to non-compliance. There'd be no material breaching here, by God! Ms Amanda Lenville had a job to do, and she intended to do it.

And so, in the interest of saving her dignity, Amanda drew a deep breath, stayed her still-pulsing organs with a well-placed hand to the stomach, and opened her eyes to confront her host.

Unfortunately, what her eyes discovered was neither Saddam (nor, it has to be said, any accepted form of dignity), but the huge and pressing face of the principal Palace guard. A grizzled, sneering man, he had moved, while she'd been pondering, to within inches of her face, and was ogling her unrepentantly.

Amanda flushed with discomfort at the intensity of this unwelcome attention, and was about to object when he drew back and hollered toward his comrades in arms in Arabic.

The guards exploded into raucous laughter, and their captain – having, evidently, wrapped up his work at the table – smugly retired to the remoter fringes of the room, taking the rest of them with him as he went. Amanda watched them go, then wheeled back upon Saddam, who appeared to be struggling with a strained smile of his own.

'Pray tell, Mr Hussein,' she inveighed, 'what do your praetorians have to say about the situation?'

'Ah,' the despot stumbled in return, 'at last the lady speaks! And she wishes to know about the Fedayeen? Er… he suggests – rather indelicately, I'm afraid – that, to the untrained eye, it might appear your interests here are those of a… shall we say… venereal, as much as a vocational, nature.'

His composure now restored, Saddam raised his unibrow archly. 'You must accept my apologies for his insolence.'

Amanda was indignant. How dare these men, how dare this dollar-rate dictator, presume she'd been seduced by a porn-star moustache and a plateful of oysters? Her dark eyes flashed, and her tone turned bitter.

'Forgiveness passes between friends, Mr Hussein. As we are only the barest of acquaintances, perhaps it's best we proceed to the business at hand.'

A moment passed before Saddam could summon a reply. When he did, his voice was contrite, and his manner deferential. 'Yes, of course. Please, do go on, Miss Lenville. I don't want us to –'

But Amanda stopped him before he could finish. 'To begin with, Mr Hussein, let me remind you that there is not now, nor ever will there be, any 'us' to speak of. And furthermore,' she added shrilly, attempting to stare him into submission, 'if you wish me to remain in your presence, I must insist that you refer to me as... as...'

Amanda tried to force a 'Ms' from her mouth, but none was forthcoming. Saddam had met her eyes with so wounded an aspect, so pitiful a posture (almost, she could have said, like a puppy scolded for showing affection) that, no matter how dammed up she wished to remain, all of the hardness drained from her heart.

What was more, it wasn't just her heart that softened at the sight of him: lots of her other parts were flooding as well. And with good cause! Amanda thought, licking her lips as she moved her stare from his face to the rest of his figure. Only an unsightly paunch marred the lines of his perfect physique – and not even that could keep Amanda from feeling drawn to him like super-heated plutonium penetrating a tritium core. Once again, she realized, his allure was airbursting her will to defy it.

'Oh, what's the use,' she sighed. 'Call me Amanda.'

Saddam's smile practically irradiated the room. 'And as I hope to show you later, Amanda, I am not the sort of man to take without giving. I beg of you, you must call me Saddam!'

Amanda sighed again. How could she help but believe him? His smile was so magnanimous, his body such a bountiful harvest, that suddenly she saw him as the charitable, beneficent Saddam portrayed in all of those Baghdad murals and monuments. Maybe, she surmised, in an appalling fall from feminist grace, this side of Saddam is *always* there. Maybe it simply needs the love of a good woman to coax it out!

Maybe so, Amanda brooded. But for the time being all she wanted to do was gape at the beauty of the man before her. She stared at him; he smiled on her; and together they sat, eye to bewitching eye, for what Amanda thought might be forever... until Saddam blinked.

3

With a nervous glance toward the back of the room, where his guards sat smoking and shooting dice, Saddam broke the enchanted silence with a whisper. 'Perhaps it really is best,' he counselled, conspiratorially, 'that you proceed with your questions, as planned.'

Had Amanda been better aware of her surroundings, she might have noticed something odd about Saddam's secretive behavior. As things stood, however, she couldn't see past the mystery of the one discrepancy, the one miraculous inconsistency, which overrode all others.

Here she was, after all, on assignment in deepest darkest, about-to-be-invaded Iraq, completely surrounded by heat-packing anti-American zealots who, when they weren't laughing in her face, were probably itching to pump her full of lead (and God knew what besides). And yet, in spite of everything, she felt completely right with the world – completely right, she knew, because *he* was there.

Next to such a paradox, Saddam's request to move forward with an already-scheduled interview seemed nothing short of perfectly reasonable. Happy to honour it, Amanda rummaged blithely though her papers and, locating the list of questions she'd prepared in advance, fired away from the top.

'Tell me, Saddam, about your childhood. How would you say it helped to mould you into the man you are today?' She felt silly talking this way, almost as though she were making conversation on a first date.

Saddam, however, took the question seriously. 'You will have heard many things about my youth, I expect. That I was an orphan, perhaps, or a runaway? Myself, I usually say it was the call to sacrifice that seized me away from my family and brought me to the feet of my uncle in Baghdad.

'My 'uncle',' he went on, his voice laced with venom, 'has made me everything you see today. What I've learned of statesmanship, of politics and battle, I have learned from him.'

Saddam paused a moment, then recovered his smile as he

leaned in toward Amanda. 'What I've learned of love, however, is a different story. Of love, the sacred texts have taught me. I have had to learn from Solomon, from Scheherazade and Shakespeare. From Sinatra,' he continued, nodding toward the speakers over-head, 'and, of course,' he finished, his fingers moving noticeably toward his bulging crotch, 'from your news broadcasts.'

Amanda's pulse quickened dramatically: even Saddam's sleazy come-ons were arousing her now. She forced herself to breathe deeply before blurting out her follow-up. 'How do you put these lessons to work, when performing your public duties as President of Iraq?'

'You can be assured, Amanda,' Saddam returned, arching his eyebrow once more, 'that each of my subjects receives my full devotion as a public servant. I pump myself to the bone ensuring that every last drop of my toil, my tears, my sweat, and my blood – for those who like that sort of thing – is spent in the pursuit of their happiness.'

Amanda's aorta chattered away at Geiger-counter intensity. Gulping audibly, she put aside her papers and asked the only fur-ther question she could bring to mind. 'And what do you do,' she stammered, in a small voice, 'with your private time?'

'Really, Amanda, I have none,' Saddam replied.

'Most of your hours are given to government affairs, then?'

'It is true what you say, but there is more than that alone. The life I lead now – its power, prestige, its extravagance – it has cost me much, Amanda. To keep it I have had to surrender my dreams of private passion. I have had to act, at all times, with only public motives in mind. Living this way has been difficult, but I have managed it. I have simply told myself: to do differently, is to give oneself over to years of torture. It is to sell oneself short, to cast oneself into the clutches of the Man.

'I have believed this almost all my life. I believed it when I was young, and understood, for the first time, that I would never see my parents again. I believed it this morning, when I woke and took my breakfast. I believed it on the way down the stairs to meet you. But now, Amanda,' he concluded, meaningfully brushing his hand against hers, 'I do not know if I can believe it any longer.'

Amanda felt that she might swoon.

'Look,' she gasped. 'I can't keep doing this.'

'This?'

'This... this double-talking, this misdirection. Saddam, I've got to know: Why am I here? Why not Dan Rather? Why me? Why all this?' she questioned, gesturing toward the table, the music, the elegant room around them. 'Why *this*?' she added, referring to his eager hand as it probed at her dress and inner thighs.

Saddam stilled his probing and pronounced, after a moment's pensive silence: 'You ask me, what is this? Well I ask *you*, Amanda, what is *this*?' He gestured in circles about the space around them. 'This free food, these fine garments, the thousands of beautiful girls who grovel and writhe before me in the market-place? What, I ask, is *any* of it without love?

'And yet, for nothing more than this I have pimped my very spirit, Amanda. For this I have lived a thousand schedules like the one I read you now.'

Reaching into his jacket pocket, Saddam withdrew what looked like a business card. He translated it aloud.

'5:00am: Meet with impressionable young American journalist.

'5:30am: Escort impressionable young American journalist to Room 6.

'5:45am: Meet with French delegation.'

Saddam returned the schedule to his pocket and drew himself up in his chair. 'But now I... well, I don't *want* to meet with the French delegation. I want...'

He paused, and looked at her imploringly. 'Don't you see what I am trying to say, Amanda?'

Amanda sat silently, fain but flummoxed.

'Very well, then,' he sighed. 'You shall hear the answers you have asked for.'

He spoke quickly now, but quietly, under his breath. 'I am not Saddam Hussein. The real Saddam is old and fat, does not speak English. My name is Moshi al-Harith. I am French Algerian; I was kidnapped here away from my family as a boy. By accident I looked like Saddam so they made me one of his doubles – into a procurer, by trade.

'I am ashamed to admit it, but you have been brought here to preserve the power and privilege of which I have spoken. It was thought that I could offer you a taste of this privilege; that with a little food, a lot of fine wine, and maybe a trip to the President's... how do you say it... 'fuck pad' (where he, not I, would do the honours), we could solicit your influence, and have you tell your countrymen, 'Saddam Hussein, he is no bad guy. He is a man who feels for his people.'

Moshi replaced his hand on Amanda's leg, as though to drive the point home. 'The plan was, you would stand atop the Palestine Hotel and say to the world, 'this regime does not need changing.''

Amanda knew that she should vent and rage, that she should rise and storm away resentfully – but she also knew she lacked conviction. She was welded to her seat, transfixed by the magic of Moshi's confession.

'There is more to say,' he continued. 'I cannot expect you will believe me, yet still it is true. I have told you, I came here to do a job, and the job was going well. Everything was normal. But then something happened. I don't know exactly how, or when, or why, but somewhere along the way we met – not as a government official and his guest, not as a reporter and her subject – but as linked and kindred souls. Yes, Amanda, our souls have met: not alone across this table, but across what seem eternities. Our souls make love: not alone right now nor later, cheaply, in Room 6, but across untold infinities.

'So you see, Amanda: what started as a falsehood, has become a revelation. What was meant to send a message, became all about the messenger. You, Ms Amanda Lenville of America and CNN, have caused, and not discouraged, a regime change in Iraq today. You have caused a regime change... in my heart.'

Moshi stood abruptly and held out his hands. 'I will take you upstairs, Amanda,' he whispered, 'where we will be together. They will kill me if we are caught... but I do not care. I throw away all cares, I spit on my life. Everything I have ever done, everything they can ever do to me, is nothing next to a single second in your arms.'

Amanda took his arm and climbed the stairs beside him, impervious to the licentious grins of the guards below. She was aware of nothing now; only that her soul felt prepped to leave the silo where so long she had confined it; that she was rocketing toward freedom; that she was going ballistic and *liking* it; that her body cried out for impact with its target of desire.

But when they reached Room 6; when Moshi escorted Amanda through the door and slid the lock shut behind them, there was no time for precision targeting. The lovers met in a mad caress, carpeting each other with strikes from lips and tongue. Amanda tore wildly at Moshi's shirt and tie, running her eager, searching hands down his frontside, arresting them only when they encountered the firmness of his paunch.

Moshi, his diction muffled by the folds of her dress in his teeth, acknowledged Amanda's hesitancy with a smirk. 'There is something more you should know,' he pronounced, pushing her back to a distance. In a single fluid motion, he tore the paunch away from his person and heaved it to the floor, revealing a rippling set of abs and, what was better, the throbbing proof that his firmness was more than prosthetic plastic.

Amanda's womanhood ached with apprehension: Moshi was, both inside and out, the most beautiful man she'd ever seen. She wanted to be 80,000 slaves and 72 virgins to him all at once. She yearned to burn from the blast of his cock, to fuel the fires she knew his jumbo jet would visit upon her.

Launching herself across the room, she tackled Moshi to the floor and they met once more, their bodies buckling like steel girders twisted in a molten, imploding embrace. The walls reverberated with the intensity of their undulations, rumbling at first, then rattling and roaring until finally – in a moment of massive release – the universe seemed to detonate, linking them both in a nirvanic, eternal instant of abandon.

It took Amanda some time, once she'd slithered free of Moshi's ministrations, to realize that the explosion she'd absorbed was a part of the real, and not just her sexual, world. Shattered glass littered the rug she was lying on. Thick black smoke poured over the palace rooftops. Heavy steps echoed on the stairwell, and the door burst open behind her.

The captain of the guards rushed in and shouted in Arabic. At his words, a company of Fedayeen charged past their master and into the room. Four of them seized Amanda, whose modesty had compelled her to pull her abaaya up from her ankles instead of trying to escape. With Moshi, however, they weren't so fortunate. The last thing Amanda saw – before her captors cloaked her vision with a black and rough-hewn hood – was her half-naked lover, breaking free of his assailants and plunging through the nearest window, sprinting away toward where, she realized, her jeep must be parked. In the darkness, Amanda cried out, and struggled to join him.

She was rewarded for her efforts with a rifle butt to the back of the head.

4

For Amanda, whose morning had become an exercise in seguing from one ridiculous state of consciousness into another, this latest transition was the worst by far. Only seconds ago, she'd been floating in a state of lustful fantasia. Now, she found herself suffocated by a burlap bag, restrained by guards she couldn't see, crippled by a gratuitous clobbering, and – worst of all – beset by recriminations which swelled with the pain from the base of her skull.

'Damn it all!' she rued. 'The bastard up and ran off without me! He probably never cared for me to begin with – just saw me as a piece of ass with a jeep and a Western passport: the perfect ticket out of this place. And even if he did care for me, even if his love were real, what was I ever going to do with it? Smuggle him back to the States? Live with him in Washington, happily ever after twenty years of CIA analysis determined that he wasn't, in fact, the real Saddam? Christ, what a fool I've been!'

But then, in spite of herself, she began to remember Moshi's finer points: his eyes, his smile, his magnificent phallus. 'Who am I kidding?' she relented, weeping softly. 'I was a fool, it's true; but I'm *still* a fool even now. I'd give anything to see him here, anything to hold him again and never let go.'

No sooner had she made this wish than, without warning, her captors skittered away from her side, casting her loose as they went. Amanda ripped the hood from her head and squinted, straining to adjust to the light. Wait a minute, she puzzled: there seemed to be some sort of a commotion going on around her. But why should they be fighting? Why should they be screaming, and dashing for – WAIT A MINUTE. Was that Moshi? Was that *Moshi*, stabbing and eviscerating the guards who'd held her down? Was that Moshi, beheading their captain with a gleaming saber? Was that Moshi, dropping his sword and walking toward her...?

'Oh it is it is it is!' she exclaimed with as much excitement as her burdened mind could muster. Her sight seemed to clear with each step Moshi took her way until, before she knew it, she was back in his arms, and blinded only by love for him.

'You came back to me!' she panted, as the steaming gore from his victims smeared onto her skin.

'Amanda, you know I could never leave you,' Moshi returned, enclosing her tightly in his blood-and-brain-stained biceps. Leaning down, he stripped the trousers from one of the dead guards, held them up to his waist to check their length, and donned them over his nakedness, tucking in his shirt with the air of a job well done.

'Your jeep,' he said, as the song of an approaching siren teased at Amanda's ears, 'has been destroyed in the American attack.'

'But not to worry,' he went on, his eyes all a-twinkle. 'I have met with the French delegation after all. Amanda, they are coming for us. They are coming to take a son of the Motherland – and a daughter of Venus – back to the place where they both belong.'

With this, Moshi delicately lifted Amanda off her feet, and carried her out to the courtyard. He pointed her exhausted head toward the site of the blast, whence the smoke was billowing, and whither the soldiers were bearing. Out of the whirling blackness came a long limousine, moving swiftly toward them. Its twin *tricoleurs* waved bravely in the breeze.

Amanda smiled at the sight, and nuzzled Moshi appreciatively. She recognized, in the nasal *oui ouah* of the staff car's siren, the promise of flight from this fighting – of flight from *all* of it, not just the death and destruction in Baghdad, but the war she'd waged against herself and her instincts, over so many years of strict self-denial.

The car closed in. It came to a stop, and the door opened, to her and to Moshi. By the time she was hoisted inside; by the time the door had shut and the motor had whirred and they were underway, Amanda's eyes were closed. She drifted off, and she dreamt – finally and for the first time – the dream all good girls dream: a dream of princes, of forbidden passion, and the inevitability of Paris in the spring.

Biographical Notes

Ruth Thomas is the author of two short story collections, *Sea Monster Tattoo*, shortlisted for the *Mail on Sunday*/John Llewellyn Rhys Prize for Fiction and the Saltire First Book award, and *The Dance Settee* (both Polygon). Her work also appears regularly on the BBC. Based in Edinburgh, she has just completed a third short story collection and is now writing a novel.

Rob Tomlinson is from Nottingham, England. For sixteen years he worked as a reporter on regional newspapers and variously as a reporter, producer, newsreader and presenter for BBC Radio and ITV. In 2002 he took a break from his career to do a Masters degree in Creative Writing at Edinburgh University. He currently lives in Edinburgh and is working on his first novel.

Dilys Rose lives in Edinburgh. Her previous publications include the short story collections *Our Lady of the Pickpockets*, *Red Tides* – shortlisted for the McVitie's Scottish Writer of the Year and the Saltire Scottish Book of the Year – and *War Dolls*; she has also had published a novel, *Pest Maiden*, nominated for the Impac prize; and the poetry collection *Madame Doubtfire's Dilemma*. A new collection of poetry, *Lure,* is due out soon (Chapman). She is currently Writer in Residence at Edinburgh University.

Aury Wallington is a writer on the Emmy-winning HBO programme *Sex and the City*. She was the winner of the 1999 MTV Fiction Writing contest, and her story 'Day of the Dead' appears in the book *Pieces, a Collection of New Voices* (Pocket Books 2000). She wrote the pilot for *The Safety Zone*, a new cable show produced by Amani Entertainment, and her feature film script, *Page Six*, was optioned by Pipe Dream Productions. She has worked in a variety of capacities on films including *Analyze This*, *Sunburn*, *Freak*, *Lulu on the Bridge*, *The Street*, *Cold Feet*, *Spawn* and *Body Count*. Her freelance writing credits include Benzo, Writer's Digest, BUST, Scriptwriting Secrets, Guava, mediabistro.com and HBO.com.

Ken Shand lives in Glasgow and recently completed a Masters in Creative Writing at the University of Edinburgh. His stories and poems have been published in various magazines round Scotland. He recently won the Sloane Prize for a poem he wrote in Lowland Scots.

Kate Tregaskis graduated from Newcastle Polytechnic's Fine Art degree course in 1988 and then taught photography to various community groups before co-founding Zone Gallery in Newcastle upon Tyne in 1991. From 1995 to 2001 she was Artistic Director at Stills Gallery in Edinburgh. She left to enroll on the MLitt Creative Writing Course at Glasgow and Strathclyde Universities and subsequently on the MSc in Creative Writing at Edinburgh University. In 2001 she took part in Critical Voices, a project involving 50 writers initiated by the Arts Council for the Republic of Ireland. In 2002 she was awarded a New Writers Bursary from the Scottish Arts Council and was shortlisted for the regional final of the Real Writers Short Story Awards. Her work appears in an anthology of new Scottish writing entitled *A Fictional Guide to Scotland*. She lives and works in Edinburgh.

Evan Rosenthal was born and raised in Cleveland, Ohio, USA. He graduated from Washington University in St. Louis in 2000 and moved to New York City where he worked as a financial analyst and part-time screenwriter. After two years in Manhattan he relocated to Scotland, enrolling in the Masters program in Creative Writing at the University of Edinburgh and is now writing his first novel. He is the creator and co-editor of *Outlandish Affairs*.

Liz Berry recently completed her undergraduate degree in English Literature and English Language at the University of Edinburgh. She has published poetry in a number of journals, written two plays for London radio stations and in 1996 had a play produced at the Battersea Arts Centre as part of the Woolwich Young Radio Playwrights Award. In 2001 she wrote and directed a play for the Bedlam Festival of New Theatre in Scotland. She is currently concentrating on poetry which she also enjoys performing. Liz works with primary school children with language impairments and hopes to go on to train as a primary school teacher.

Amanda Robinson has lived on both sides of the Atlantic and is co-editor of *Outlandish Affairs*. She worked for several years as a graphic designer in London before moving north to pursue a Masters degree in Creative Writing at the University of Edinburgh. She is currently based in the Scottish Borders and writing her first novel.

Suhayl Saadi is an internationally-published, award-winning short-story writer and novelist. He received a Millennium Commission Award in 1999, and in 2002, he edited *Macallan/ Scotland on Sunday Shorts 5*. He has worked on the Literature Committee of the Scottish Arts Council, and has performed readings of his work in New York and in Brussels, as well as appearing fre-quently on BBC Radio. His work has been published in places as disparate as San Diego, Karachi, Barcelona and Slovenia and he has worked on various projects with writers/artists from Syria, Croatia, India and Germany. He has written radio-plays for BBC Radio 4, one of which will be broadcast in 2004. His own short story collection, *The Burning Mirror* was short-listed for the Saltire First Book Prize, and a novel, *Psychoraag*, is due out in 2004 (Black and White Publishing). www.suhaylsaadi.com

Curt Rosenthal was born and raised in Cleveland, Ohio, USA and now lives in New York. He has lived, written, worked and taught in places as diverse as Africa, Chicago and Israel, with a stint as a professional footballer in Holland. He has written various screen-plays and holds a degree in English Literature from Miami University. He is currently enrolled in the Creative Writing MFA program at Antioch University.

Marcie Hume was born in Boulder, Colorado, USA. She graduated from Vassar College and holds a MSc with Distinction in Creative Writing from the University of Edinburgh. Her work has appeared in *Into the Teeth of the Wind*, published by the University of California at Santa Barbara, and *Nomad Magazine*, published by Edinburgh University. She worked for several years in off-Broadway theatre in New York City, and currently lives in Reykjavik, Iceland.

Joshua Isard is a native of Philadelphia, Pennsylvania. He has studied at the George Washington University, Temple University, and the University of Edinburgh. He is now working on his first novel.

Aimee Chalmers has had poetry and prose published in literary magazines in Scots and English, and recently completed an MPhil in Creative Writing at Glasgow University and plans to begin a Creative Writing PhD on 'Creativity as an Expression of Longing' based on the lives of the Angus Poets. She is a member of the Society of Authors and is on the Scottish Writers' Register.

Brian D. Algra is a native of Los Angeles, California, and the owner of a Harvard-trained mind. His undergraduate thesis was not sufficiently excruciating to keep him from attempting a PhD at the University of Edinburgh, where he is enrolled as a student of English and American Literature. Brian has been published as – among other things – a poet, sportswriter, political columnist, travel expert, book reviewer, film enthusiast and theatre critic. He has also tried his hand at screenwriting and absurdist drama and hopes to continue moulding himself into a modern-day man of letters.

Some other books published by **LUATH** PRESS

But n Ben A-Go-Go
Matthew Fitt
ISBN 1 84282 041 1 PB £6.99

The year is 2090. Global flooding has left most of Scotland under water. The descendants of those who survived God's Flood live in a community of floating island parishes, known collectively as Port. Port's citizens live in mortal fear of Senga, a supervirus whose victims are kept in a giant hospital warehouse in sealed capsules called Kists. Paolo Broon is a low-ranking cyberjanny. His life-partner, Nadia, lies forgotten and alone in Omega Kist 624 in the Rigo Imbeki Medical Center. When he receives an unexpected message from his radge criminal father to meet him at But n Ben A-Go-Go, Paolo's life is changed forever. He must traverse VINE, Port and the Drylands and deal with rebel American tourists and crabbit Dundonian microchips to discover the truth about his family's past in order to free Nadia from the sair grip of the merciless Senga. Set in a distinctly unbonnie future-Scotland, the novel's dangerous atmosphere and psychologically-malkied characters weave a tale that both chills and intrigues. In *But n Ben A-Go-Go* Matthew Fitt takes the allegedly dead language of Scots and energises it with a narrative that crackles and fizzes with life.

'I recommend an entertaining and ground-breaking book.' EDWIN MORGAN

'… if you can't get hold of a copy, mug somebody'
MARK STEPHEN, SCOTTISH
CONNECTION, BBC RADIO SCOTLAND

'the last man who tried anything like this was Hugh MacDiarmid' MICHAEL FRY, TODAY
PROGRAMME, BBC RADIO 4

'going where no man has gone before'
STEPHEN NAYSMITH, SUNDAY HERALD

'Bursting with sly humour, staggeringly imaginative, often poignant and at times exploding with Uzi-blazing action, this book is a cracker… With Matthew Fitt's book I began to think and sometimes dream in Scots.' GREGOR STEELE,
TIMES EDUCATIONAL SUPPLEMENT

The Road Dance
John MacKay
ISBN 1 84282 024 9 PB £9.99

The bond between a mother and her child is the strongest in the natural world. So why would a young woman, dreaming of America, throw her newborn baby into the waves of the wild Atlantic ocean?

Life in the Scottish Hebrides can be harsh – 'The Edge of the World' some call it. For Kirsty MacLeod, the love of Murdo promises a new life away from the scrape of the land and the suppression of the church. But the Great War looms and the villages hold a grand Road Dance to send their young men off to battle. It will be matched only by the one held to welcome them home.

As the dancers swirl and sup, Kirsty is overpowered and raped by an unknown assailant. She hides her dark secret fearful of what it will mean for her and the baby she is carrying. Only the embittered doctor, a man with a cold wife and a colder bed, suspects.

On a fateful day of surging seas and swelling pain Kirsty learns that her love will never be back. Now she must make her choice and it is no choice at all.

And the hunt for the baby's mother and his killer become one and the same.

'[MacKay] has captured time, place and atmosphere superbly… a very good debut.'
MEG HENDERSON

'Powerful, shocking, heartbreaking…'
DAILY MAIL

Milk Treading
Nick Smith
ISBN 1 84282 037 0 PB £6.99

Life isn't easy for Julius Kyle, a jaded crime hack with the *Post*. When he wakes up on a sand barge with his head full of grit he knows things have to change. But how fast they'll change he doesn't guess until his best friend Mick jumps to his death off a fifty foot bridge outside the *Post*'s window. Worst of all, he's a cat. That means keeping himself scrupulously clean, defending his territory and battling an addiction to milk. He lives in Bast, a sprawling city of alleyways and claw-shaped towers... join Julius as he prowls deep into the crooked underworld of Bast, contending with political intrigue, territorial disputes and dog-burglars, murder, mystery and mayhem.

'This is certainly the only cat-centred political thriller that I've read and it has a weird charm, not to mention considerable humour...'
AL KENNEDY

'A trip into a surreal and richly-realised feline-canine world.' ELLEN GALFORD

'Milk Treading is equal parts Watership Down, Animal Farm, and The Big Sleep. A novel of class struggle, political intrigue and good old-fashioned murder and intrigue. And, oh yeah, all the characters are either cats or dogs.' TOD GOLDBERG, LAS VEGAS MERCURY

'Smith writes with wit and energy creating a memorable brood of characters...'
ALAN RADCLIFFE, THE LIST

Kitty Killer Cult
Nick Smith
ISBN 1 84282 039 7 £9.99

Clapped-out cat detective Tiger Straight investigates a series of nasty murders on his home turf of Nub City. He falls in love with Kerry, a fatal femme who works as a make-up artist on a TV show. Rival investigator Cole Tiddle and Inspector Bix Mortis follow up reports of a Kitty Killer Cult.

Tiger's partner, Bug, suspects that the Auld Enemy are at work – but dogs aren't to blame for the murders. Creatures far more insidious, far more unlikely are responsible. They won't stop until every last cat in the city is dead. Only Tiger can save his friends, but what will he have to sacrifice along the way?

The Strange Case of RL Stevenson
Richard Woodhead
ISBN 0 946487 86 3 HB £16.99

A consultant physician for 22 years with a strong interest in Robert Louis Stevenson's life and work, Richard Woodhead was intrigued by the questions raised by the references to his symptoms. The assumption that he suffered from consumption (tuberculosis) – the diagnosis of the day – is challenged in *The Strange Cast of RL Stevenson*. Dr Woodhead examines how Stevenson's life was affected by his illness and his perception of it. This fictional work puts words into the mouths of five doctors who treated RLS at different periods of his adult life. Though these doctors existed in real-life, little is documented of their private conversations with RLS. However, everything Dr Woodhead postulates could have occurred within the known framework of RLS's life. RLS's writing continues to compel readers today. The fact that he did much of his writing while confined to his sick-bed is fascinating. What illness could have contributed to his creativity?

'This pleasantly unassuming book describes the medical history of Robert Louis Stevenson through a series of fictional reminiscences... I thoroughly enjoyed it. This would make a charming gift for any enthusiastic fan of RLS.'
MEDICAL HISTORY JOURNAL

'RLS himself is very much a real figure, as is Fanny, his wife, while his parents are sympathetically and touchingly portrayed.' SCOTS MAGAZINE

'his factual research is faultless, resulting in a very good and very readable novel written in the spirit of the time... My prescription: take one of the five parts per diem as a lovely Book at Bedtime.'
BRIAN DAVIS , TIME OUT

The Great Melnikov
Hugh MacLachlan
ISBN 0 946487 42 1 PB £7.95

A well crafted, gripping novel, written in a style reminiscent of John Buchan and set in London and the Scottish Highlands during the First World War, *The Great Melnikov* is a dark tale of double-cross and deception. We first meet Melnikov, one-time star of the German circus, languishing as a down-and-out in Trafalgar Square. He soon finds himself drawn into a tortuous web of intrigue.

He is a complex man whose personal struggle with alcoholism is an inner drama which parallels the tense twists and turns as a spy mystery unfolds. Melnikov's options are narrowing.

The circle of threat is closing. Will Melnikov outwit the sinister enemy spy network? Can he summon the will and the wit to survive?

Hugh MacLachlan, in his first full length novel, demonstrates an undoubted ability to tell a good story well. His earlier stories have been broadcast on Radio Scotland, and he has the rare distinction of being shortlisted for the Macallan/Scotland on Sunday Short Story Competition two years in succession.

'*Short, sharp and to the point... racing along to a suitably cinematic ending, richly descriptive, yet clear and lean.*' THE SCOTSMAN

Driftnet
Lin Anderson
ISBN 1 84282 034 6 PB £9.99

A teenager is found strangled and mutilated in a Glasgow flat. Leaving her warm bed and lover in the middle of the night to take forensic samples from the body, Rhona MacLeod soon recognises the likeness between herself and the dead boy and is horrified to think that he might be the son she gave up for adoption seventeen years before.

Amidst the turmoil of her own love life and consumed by guilt from her past, Rhona sets out to find both the boy's killer and her own son. But the powerful men who use the Internet to trawl for vulnerable boys have nothing to lose and everything to gain by Rhona MacLeod's death.

'*Linda Anderson has a rare gift. She is one of the few able to convey urban and rural Scotland with equal truth... Compelling, vivid stuff. I couldn't put it put it down.*' ANNE MACLEOD, AUTHOR OF THE DARK SHIP

The Fundamentals of New Caledonia
David Nicol
ISBN 0 946487 93 6 HB £16.99

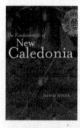

'*David Nicol takes one of the great 'what if?' moments of Scottish history, the disastrous Darien venture, and pulls the reader into this bungling, back-stabbing episode through the experiences of a time-travelling Edinburgh lad press-ganged into the service of the Scots Trading Company.*

The time-travel element, together with a sophisticated linguistic interaction between contemporary and late 17th-century Scots, signals that this is no simple reconstruction of a historical incident. The economic and social problems faced by the citizens of 'New Caledonia', battered by powerful international forces and plagued by conflict between public need and private greed, are still around 300 years on.' JAMES ROBERTSON, AUTHOR OF THE FANATIC AND JOSEPH KNIGHT

'*...a breathtaking book, sublimely streaming with adrenalin and inventiveness... Incidentally, in a work of remarkable intellectual and imaginative scope, David Nicol has achieved some of the most deliciously erotic sequences ever written in Scots.*' JENNIE RENTON, EDITOR, SCOTTISH BOOK COLLECTOR

FICTION

Six Black Candles
Des Dillon
ISBN 1 84282 053 2 PB £6.99

Me and My Gal
Des Dillon
ISBN 1 84282 054 0 PB £5.99

The Bannockburn Years
William Scott
ISBN 0 946487 34 0 PB £7.95

POETRY

Drink the Green Fairy
Brian Whittingham
ISBN 1 84282 020 6 PB £8.99

The Ruba'iyat of Omar Khayyam, in Scots
Rab Wilson
ISBN 1 84282 046 X PB £8.99

Talking with Tongues
Brian Finch
ISBN 1 84282 006 0 PB £8.99

Kate o Shanter's Tale and other poems [book]
Matthew Fitt
ISBN 1 84282 028 1 PB £6.99

Kate o Shanter's Tale and other poems [audio CD]
Matthew Fitt
ISBN 1 84282 043 5 PB £9.99

Bad Ass Raindrop
Kokumo Rocks
ISBN 1 84282 018 4 PB £6.99

Madame Fifi's Farewell and other poems
Gerry Cambridge
ISBN 1 84282 005 2 PB £8.99

Scots Poems to be Read Aloud
intro Stuart McHardy
ISBN 0 946487 81 2 PB £5.00

Picking Brambles
Des Dillon
ISBN 1 84282 021 4 PB £6.99

Sex, Death & Football
Alistair Findlay
ISBN 1 84282 022 2 PB £6.99

Tartan and Turban
Bashabi Fraser
ISBN 1 84282 044 3 PB £8.99

Immortal Memories: A Compilation of Toasts to the Memory of Burns as delivered at Burns Suppers, 1801-2001
John Cairney
ISBN 1 84282 009 5 HB £20.00

Poems to be Read Aloud
introduced by Tom Atkinson
ISBN 0 946487 00 6 PB £5.00

Men and Beasts: wild men and tame animals
Valerie Gillies and Rebecca Marr
ISBN 0 946487 92 8 PB £15.00

FOLKLORE

Scotland: Myth, Legend & Folklore
Stuart McHardy
ISBN 0 946487 69 3 PB £7.99

Luath Storyteller: Highland Myths & Legends
George W Macpherson
ISBN 1 84282 003 6 PB £5.00

Tales of the North Coast
Alan Temperley
ISBN 0 946487 18 9 PB £8.99

Tall Tales from an Island
Peter Macnab
ISBN 0 946487 07 3 PB £8.99

The Supernatural Highlands
Francis Thompson
ISBN 0 946487 31 6 PB £8.99

CARTOONS

Broomie Law
Cinders McLeod
ISBN 0 946487 99 5 PB £4.00

THE QUEST FOR

The Quest for Robert Louis Stevenson
John Cairney
ISBN 0 946487 87 1 HB £16.99

The Quest for the Nine Maidens
Stuart McHardy
ISBN 0 946487 66 9 HB £16.99

The Quest for the Original Horse Whisperers
Russell Lyon
ISBN 1 842820 020 6 HB £16.99

The Quest for the Celtic Key
Karen Ralls-MacLeod and
Ian Robertson
ISBN 0 946487 73 1 HB £18.99
ISBN 1 84282 031 1 PB £8.99

The Quest for Arthur
Stuart McHardy
ISBN 1 842820 12 5 HB £16.99

ON THE TRAIL OF

On the Trail of William Wallace
David R Ross
ISBN 0 946487 47 2 PB £7.99

On the Trail of Robert the Bruce
David R Ross
ISBN 0 946487 52 9 PB £7.99

On the Trail of Mary Queen of Scots
J Keith Cheetham
ISBN 0 946487 50 2 PB £7.99

On the Trail of Bonnie Prince Charlie
David R Ross
ISBN 0 946487 68 5 PB £7.99

On the Trail of Robert Burns
John Cairney
ISBN 0 946487 51 0 PB £7.99

On the Trail of John Muir
Cherry Good
ISBN 0 946487 62 6 PB £7.99

On the Trail of Queen Victoria in the Highlands
Ian R Mitchell
ISBN 0 946487 79 0 PB £7.99

On the Trail of Robert Service
G Wallace Lockhart
ISBN 0 946487 24 3 PB £7.99

On the Trail of the Pilgrim Fathers
J Keith Cheetham
ISBN 0 946487 83 9 PB £7.99

On the Trail of John Wesley
J Keith Cheetham
ISBN 1 84282 023 0 PB £7.99

On the Trail of Scotland's Myths & Legends
Stuart McHardy
ISBN 1 84282 049 4 PB £7.99

LUATH GUIDES TO SCOTLAND

The North West Highlands: Roads to the Isles
Tom Atkinson
ISBN 0 946487 54 5 PB £4.95

Mull and Iona: Highways and Byways
Peter Macnab
ISBN 0 946487 58 8 PB £4.95

The Northern Highlands: The Empty Lands
Tom Atkinson
ISBN 0 946487 55 3 PB £4.95

The West Highlands: The Lonely Lands
Tom Atkinson
ISBN 0 946487 56 1 PB £4.95

HISTORY

Scots in Canada
Jenni Calder
ISBN 1 84282 038 9 PB £7.99

Civil Warrior
Robin Bell
ISBN 1 84282 013 3 HB £10.99

A Passion for Scotland
David R Ross
ISBN 1 84282 019 2 PB £5.99

Reportage Scotland
Louise Yeoman
ISBN 0 946487 61 8 PB £9.99

Blind Harry's Wallace
Hamilton of Gilbertfield
[introduced by Elspeth King]
ISBN 0 946487 33 2 PB £8.99

**Plaids & Bandanas: Highland
Drover to Wild West Cowboy**
Rob Gibson
ISBN 0 946487 88 X PB £7.99

**Napiers History of Herbal
Healing, Ancient and Modern**
Tom Atkinson
ISBN 1 84282 025 7 HB £16.99

POLITICS & CURRENT ISSUES

Scotlands of the Mind
Angus Calder
ISBN 1 84282 008 7 PB £9.99

**Trident on Trial: the case for
people's disarmament**
Angie Zelter
ISBN 1 84282 004 4 PB £9.99

**Uncomfortably Numb: A Prison
Requiem**
Maureen Maguire
ISBN 1 84282 001 X PB £8.99

**Scotland: Land & Power – the
Agenda for Land Reform**
Andy Wightman
ISBN 0 946487 70 7 PB £5.00

Old Scotland New Scotland
Jeff Fallow
ISBN 0 946487 40 5 PB £6.99

**Some Assembly Required: Behind
the scenes at the Re-birth of the
Scottish Parliament**
David Shepherd
ISBN 0 946487 84 7 PB £7.99

**Notes from the North
Incorporating a brief history of
the Scots and the English**
Emma Wood
ISBN 0 946487 46 4 PB £8.99

**Scotlands of the Future:
sustainability in a small nation**
ed Eurig Scandrett
ISBN 1 84282 035 4 PB £7.99

**Eurovision or American Dream?
Britain, the Euro and the Future
of Europe**
David Purdy
ISBN 1 84282 036 2 PB £3.99

NATURAL WORLD

**The Hydro Boys: pioneers of
renewable energy**
Emma Wood
ISBN 1 84282 047 8 PB £16.99

Wild Scotland
James McCarthy
ISBN 0 946487 37 5 PB £8.99

**Wild Lives: Otters – On the Swirl
of the Tide**
Bridget MacCaskill
ISBN 0 946487 67 7 PB £9.99

Wild Lives: Foxes – The Blood is Wild
Bridget MacCaskill
ISBN 0 946487 71 5 PB £9.99

Scotland – Land & People: An Inhabited Solitude
James McCarthy
ISBN 0 946487 57 X PB £7.99

The Highland Geology Trail
John L Roberts
ISBN 0 946487 36 7 PB £4.99

Red Sky at Night
John Barrington
ISBN 0 946487 60 X PB £8.99

Listen to the Trees
Don MacCaskill
ISBN 0 946487 65 0 PB £9.99

WALK WITH LUATH

Skye 360: walking the coastline of Skye
Andrew Dempster
ISBN 0 946487 85 5 PB £8.99

Walks in the Cairngorms
Ernest Cross
ISBN 0 946487 09 X PB £4.95

Short Walks in the Cairngorms
Ernest Cross
ISBN 0 946487 23 5 PB £4.95

The Joy of Hillwalking
Ralph Storer
ISBN 0 946487 28 6 PB £7.50

Scotland's Mountains before the Mountaineers
Ian R Mitchell
ISBN 0 946487 39 1 PB £9.99

Mountain Days and Bothy Nights
Dave Brown and Ian R Mitchell
ISBN 0 946487 15 4 PB £7.50

Mountain Outlaw
Ian R. Mitchell
ISBN 1 84282 027 3 PB £6.50

SPORT

Ski & Snowboard Scotland
Hilary Parke
ISBN 0 946487 35 9 PB £6.99

Over the Top with the Tartan Army
Andy McArthur
ISBN 0 946487 45 6 PB £7.99

SOCIAL HISTORY

Pumpherston: the story of a shale oil village
Sybil Cavanagh
ISBN 1 84282 011 7 HB £17.99
ISBN 1 84282 015 X PB £7.99

Shale Voices
Alistair Findlay
ISBN 0 946487 78 2 HB £17.99
ISBN 0 946487 63 4 PB £10.99

A Word for Scotland
Jack Campbell
ISBN 0 946487 48 0 PB £12.99

TRAVEL & LEISURE

Die Kleine Schottlandfibel [Scotland Guide in German]
Hans-Walter Arends
ISBN 0 946487 89 8 PB £8.99

Let's Explore Edinburgh Old Town
Anne Bruce English
ISBN 0 946487 98 7 PB £4.99

Let's Explore Berwick Upon Tweed
Anne Bruce English
ISBN 1 84282 029 X PB £4.99

Luath Press Limited
committed to publishing well written books worth reading

LUATH PRESS takes its name from Robert Burns, whose little collie Luath (*Gael*, swift or nimble) tripped up Jean Armour at a wedding and gave him the chance to speak to the woman who was to be his wife and the abiding love of his life. Burns called one of *The Twa Dogs* Luath after Cuchullin's hunting dog in *Ossian's Fingal*. Luath Press was established in 1981 in the heart of Burns country, and is now based a few steps up the road from Burns' first lodgings on Edinburgh's Royal Mile. Luath offers you distinctive writing with a hint of unexpected pleasures.

Most bookshops in the UK, the US, Canada, Australia, New Zealand and parts of Europe either carry our books in stock or can order them for you. To order direct from us, please send a £sterling cheque, postal order, international money order or your credit card details (number, address of cardholder and expiry date) to us at the address below. Please add post and packing as follows: UK – £1.00 per delivery address; overseas surface mail – £2.50 per delivery address; overseas airmail – £3.50 for the first book to each delivery address, plus £1.00 for each additional book by airmail to the same address. If your order is a gift, we will happily enclose your card or message at no extra charge.

Luath Press Limited
543/2 Castlehill
The Royal Mile
Edinburgh EH1 2ND
Scotland
Telephone: 0131 225 4326 (24 hours)
Fax: 0131 225 4324
email: gavin.macdougall@luath.co.uk
Website: www.luath.co.uk

ILLUSTRATION: IAN KELLAS

Edinburgh's Historic Mile
Duncan Priddle
ISBN 0 946487 97 9 PB £2.99

Pilgrims in the Rough: St Andrews beyond the 19th hole
Michael Tobert
ISBN 0 946487 74 X PB £7.99

LANGUAGE

Luath Scots Language Learner [Book]
L Colin Wilson
ISBN 0 946487 91 X PB £9.99

Luath Scots Language Learner [Double Audio CD Set]
L Colin Wilson
ISBN 1 84282 026 5 CD £16.99

FOOD & DRINK

The Whisky Muse: Scotch whisky in poem & song
various, edited by Robin Laing
ISBN 1 84282 041 9 PB £7.99

First Foods Fast: how to prepare good simple meals for your baby
Lara Boyd
ISBN 1 84282 002 8 PB £4.99

Edinburgh and Leith Pub Guide
Stuart McHardy
ISBN 0 946487 80 4 PB £4.95

BIOGRAPHY

The Last Lighthouse
Sharma Krauskopf
ISBN 0 946487 96 0 PB £7.99

Tobermory Teuchter
Peter Macnab
ISBN 0 946487 41 3 PB £7.99

Bare Feet and Tackety Boots
Archie Cameron
ISBN 0 946487 17 0 PB £7.95

Come Dungeons Dark
John Taylor Caldwell
ISBN 0 946487 19 7 PB £6.95

GENEALOGY

Scottish Roots: step-by-step guide for ancestor hunters
Alwyn James
ISBN 1 84282 007 9 PB £9.99

WEDDINGS, MUSIC AND DANCE

The Scottish Wedding Book
G Wallace Lockhart
ISBN 1 84282 010 9 PB £12.99

DANCE

Fiddles and Folk
G Wallace Lockhart
ISBN 0 946487 38 3 PB £7.95

Highland Balls and Village Halls
G Wallace Lockhart
ISBN 0 946487 12 X PB £6.95